Sunset Val

or,

The Pirate Queen
of the
Seven Skies

A thrilling account
of her first adventures
in her own words

as transcribed by

R.M.St.Martin, esq.

Published by:

Weird & Wondrous Books
85 Elgin Cres. Unit 566
Beaconsfield, QC CANADA
H9W 2B3
http://www.weirdandwondrousbooks.com

Copyright © 2010 Rob St.Martin
All rights reserved
1st printing - July 2010
Cover Art Copyright © Rob St.Martin
Interior Art Copyright © Karine Charlebois

ISBN 978-0-9866531-0-0

For my parents

Chapter One

I Am Saved From Detention With A Gopher

I know what you're going to say. 'No way, you're making this all up.' But I swear, everything I'm going to tell you is absolutely true.

"Miss Ventura?"

It's not like I was ignoring him. Not really. And I knew how he saw me: a girl with longish dark red hair staring out the window again, one hand propping up her freckled cheek. Sitting at the back of the classroom, hoping to be ignored. But Mr. Carter never ignored me. It's not like he picked on me or anything, at least, not any more than he picked on the other kids in my math class, but well...

My classmates ignored me. This was nothing new, I'm always drifting off in math class. Some of them rolled their eyes, knowing Mr. Carter would wait until he had my full attention again. He was a patient man, usually, and I knew he had dealt with daydreamers before because he'd told me over and over again, but something about me drove him crazy. Like it's my fault that I'm one of the brightest kids in his class, always scoring in the top three on exams or assignments? Maybe that's why my daydreaming in class gets him so crazy. Maybe it was the fact that I never cared that I made the top three, and really totally didn't care if I was first or third.

He was a short, chubby man with curly light brown hair, a thick moustache, glasses, and a high, nasal voice which tended to sputter like a startled gopher whenever he got angry. He waddled down the aisle between the desks toward me. The other students turned to watch the show.

I know I'm small for my age but I try to make up for it by being big on personality. I'm usually dressed in black, like I was that day: a black short sleeved button-up shirt and a wide black tie, a black and white plaid skirt worn over black leggings and black high top sneakers. Not because I'm emo or anything. I just like wearing black. It goes with everything, so I never really have to waste time wondering what to wear in the morning.

Mr. Carter stopped right in front of my desk, crossing his arms, which only added to the generally gopherish qualities of his appearance. "Valerie."

Okay, so maybe by that point I was deliberately ignoring him. I admit it, okay? Despite himself, he glanced out the window to see what was so fascinating, knowing he wouldn't see what I saw, lost in my own head again. Mostly. At least, for the last fifteen minutes or so.

He leaned down, putting his hands on my desk, and stated very clearly, "Valerie Victoria Ventura. Earth to Val, come in Val."

The other kids snickered and giggled. They'd only known me for two years, ever since my family and I moved into town. They knew this was a mild case of me drifting off. One teacher had actually knocked on my head lightly to get my attention. But I have big important thoughts, okay? And they go really deep sometimes. Sometimes when I'm lost in my head, I don't even notice hunger or thirst or any of that. This one time? I nearly passed out because I hadn't had anything to eat all day because I was thinking about how there had to be a way to avoid ever doing laundry again.

Mr. Carter waved his hand in front of my slightly unfocused gaze. It kind of surprised me, even though I was vaguely aware he stood right in front of me, and I jumped back so suddenly my chair nearly tipped over. The only thing that kept me from losing my balance completely was the fact that I snatched Mr. Carter's thick wrist with my cat-like reflexes.

Yeah, I use phrases like 'cat-like reflexes'. I read a lot of books, and I even tried writing my own novel one time, only I got distracted. It was a really cool story, too. If I ever get around to writing it all down, I'll let you know.

"So glad you could join us," Mr. Carter smirked, pulling his arm back slowly so that I could regain my balance.

"Happy to be here, sir," I answered with a grin.

Carter's smirk turned into a frown. I knew he'd been expecting an apology, or at least the slightest hint of chagrin. "After class, Miss Ventura."

My grin faltered just a little. "Yes sir."

Mr. Carter returned to his place by the blackboard. The other kids in the classroom grinned their mocking, smirking grins at me, grins I returned without the slightest hint of embarrassment or even any indication of the tiny blooms of anger I felt. Like I was the only one to drift off in Carter's class? Jeez.

Realizing they wouldn't find the reaction they were looking for, one by one they turned back to Mr. Carter and his admittedly more than a little boring lesson.

"Gee thanks," I whispered to the girl sitting next to me.

Monica was everything I wasn't: tall, dark, and popular. Somehow, and don't ask me how, this didn't make us natural enemies. A person might expect us to get along like cats and dogs, or oil and water. Or maybe fire and water. Or even possibly fire and oil. Instead, we'd been friends since I had moved into town. Being neighbours probably had something to do with it, but Monica had lots of friends vying for her attention and collected boyfriends the way I collected anime and manga. I spent a lot of time reading; Monica spent a lot of time shopping. Monica worked out every day, even the days we had Phys. Ed.; my only voluntary physical exertion was my weekly fencing class. The mystery of our friendship perplexed even us.

"Nuh-uh, Threevee," Monica whispered. "You get your own self into these things."

"Fine." Threevee. Of the many nicknames I accumulated (Red, Hey You, my stupid brother's stupid contribution Spaz, among others) it's my second favourite, probably because only Monica used it. Like my favourite nickname, Sunset.

I'd been given that one by my uncle, Vic, after whom I was partially named. Uncle Vic met me three days after my birth. Holding the silent newborn, that is, me, (I know, shock, I was silent) the giant of a man with the ginger beard and a curly ginger hairline that had been thinly receding even then had gazed into my huge and somehow highly aware blue eyes and declared, "She's as pretty as a sunset." Ever since then he was the only one who called me Sunset. I loved him deeply and completely for it.

The bell rang and Mr. Carter's incredibly boring description of parabolas came to a merciful end. Everyone gathered up their books and headed out of class. I walked up to the teacher's desk with as much enthusiasm as a prisoner going to the gallows.

"Mind explaining to me where you were?" Mr. Carter asked, arms crossed as he leaned back in his chair.

I shrugged. I wasn't about to try to explain to the man that staring off into the space above the school parking lot had been an attempt at remaining sane. Instead, I played the 'sullen adolescent' card that seemed to work so well with all the other students. "I dunno."

He shook his head and removed his glasses, cleaning them in his shirt tail. "Val, you're a smart kid with a lot of potential. I'd hate to see that potential go to waste."

"Sorry sir."

"Don't be sorry," he said. "Pay attention in class. You may not think it's important, but it is. My lectures cover things that aren't in the textbooks."

"Okay."

"Next time, I'm giving you detention. Clear?"

"Yeah."

One of his eyebrows rose in an attempt at seeming stern. It changed his appearance from 'gopher' to 'kind of like a gopher with gas.' I had to bite down on the insides of my cheeks to keep from laughing.

"Are we clear?"

"Yes, sir," I managed to say without losing it completely. "Can I go? I'll be late."

"You should have thought of that before," Mr. Carter said, turning to gather his notes and stuff them in the folder he always carried to class. He raised a paw (a hand, he raised a hand!) and waved me out of his class imperiously. "Go."

Chapter Two

Regular Life Seemed So Boring and Unfair
Before I Didn't Have One

I ran out of the classroom and down the corridor, heading for my locker to grab my history binder. I loved history class. I know, you're thinking 'What a FREAK!' But it wasn't the subject, it was the teacher. Ms. Mendez made history come alive, I swear. I quickly dialled the combination for my locker and opened the door, shoving my math books on top of the pile and rifling through the mess for my history binder and textbook. I found it just as the class-is-starting bell rang and I stopped rushing. If I was going to be late, I might as well be late.

I trailed a finger along my pride and joy – the black leather swallowtail coat I'd made from one of my Mom's old trench coats. How my mother had ever had anything so cool as a black leather trench coat, I have no idea. It had taken me months to cut and work the genuine leather, and I was justifiably proud of the result. The silver buttons running up both lapels and along the cuffs made the coat something of legend. The battered silk top hat I always wore, an inheritance from my grandfather (and it still sometimes smelled of his pipe tobacco), created my signature look, a look that made me recognizable from miles away. And hey, I was never one for fading into the crowd.

I sighed contentedly, then remembered history was my favourite class, and ran for it. Ms. Mendez greeted me with a shake of her head and a roll of her dark eyes, but didn't give me detention for being late. After all, I was her best student. It might have been a bad example for the other students, but when they had my marks (98 last term, that's an A-double-plus, thanks very much), they could be late once in a while, too.

After school, I donned my coat and hat and started walking home. It was so unfair. My family lived too close to the school to qualify for riding the school bus, but far enough away that walking home was a pain. And somehow Monica always caught a lift with one of her boyfriends, while I had to walk. She lived next door to me, for crying out loud!

Still, with my iPod firmly blasting Linkin Park into my ears, the autumn air crisp but not cold, leather jacket and silk top hat well in place, I felt a supreme contentment with my situation. Autumn was always my favourite season, even when I was a little kid. Walking home might be a pain but at least it gave me a chance to be alone. Alone with my thoughts, alone with my music, just... alone.

The trees had lost most of their leaves, making the suburbs around the school a patchwork of golds and reds and greens fading to browns and tans. Trees struck grey branches at the sky. *Like the skeletal fingers of accusers from beyond the grave*, I thought, then laughed silently. How totally emo.

"Shyeah," I said, mocking the angst-ridden style of the emo kids I knew. "Whatever. SO unfair."

Soon enough the walk home was over. I unlocked the front door and entered a war zone.

My older brother Tommy was yelling at my younger sister Melanie, something about saving over one of his video games. I didn't get all the details over my iPod, and I didn't care, either. I kicked off my high tops and went up to the bedroom I shared with Mel.

On the way I passed my older sister's room, devoid of its inhabitant but still preserved for her occasional returns from college. This, I actually did think unfair. I had to share my room with Melanie while Sandra was away at college. No one was using her room. It just stood there, Sandy's stuff gathering dust. Mom even changed the sheets once a week, like someone was sleeping in them. It was ridiculous! But I knew from long experience that bringing it up would just make my parents upset. Again.

I hung my coat carefully in the closet I shared with Mel, noticing without surprise, or anything remotely beyond pure resignation, that Melanie had pushed my stuff to one side again, making her own side seem that much larger. I tossed my granddad's hat on my desk. MY desk. I had that much to myself at least.

Of course Mel usually used my desk to try on make-up, but that had lessened since Mel spilled nail polish all over one of my assignments and both Mom and Dad had freaked out at her. I guessed that I had another, oh, week or so before Melanie started laying claim to my desk again. As it was I found one of Mel's bracelets lying on top of my books. Honestly, what was wrong with her desk? It was right there, covered in her stuff. Why did she have to use mine?

At least Mel never took any of my clothes. Melanie was definitely a magpie – she preferred bright shiny colours. My perpetually black wardrobe held nothing of interest for my sister.

Supper was the usual chaos of passed dishes, conversations shouted over other conversations, and barely had the last bite been entered into mouths when people began vacating the premises of the kitchen table. Tommy didn't even wait for the last bite, shoving the last chicken nugget into his mouth as he cleared his plate into the sink.

"Thank your mother," Dad shouted at his only son before he left the room. Like Uncle Vic, his brother, Dad resembled a huge ginger-coloured bear.

Tommy spun on one socked foot and planted a crumb-encrusted kiss on Mom's cheek. "'anks ma," he mumbled around a mouth full of nugget, then washed it down with the last gulp of his milk. Honestly, Tommy went out of his way to be such a guy.

"Look at colleges!" Dad yelled at Tommy's back. My brother had inherited the red hair and pale complexion we all shared, but had somehow avoided Dad's 'big guy' genes, and instead was simply tall, lean, and pimply. He was also graduating high school. He needed to start the college application process soon or he'd miss a full semester, and then Dad's head would explode, and I refused to clean up that mess.

"Yeah yeah," Tommy called over his shoulder as he hurtled himself up the stairs to his room.

"Tommy gets his own room," I muttered to my plate, the only thing that seemed likely to listen to me. Yeah, okay, I was feeling a little sorry for myself, so sue me.

"Don't you have fencing tonight?" Mom asked as she cleared plates.

"Oh shit!" I answered, hurriedly gobbling down the last of my mashed potatoes as I carried the dish to the sink.

"Language, Val," Mom said disapprovingly. Gee, where did I learn it from, Mom?

"Yeah, language, Val," Mel mocked. I raised an eyebrow at my sister. We both knew Mel used language that was much worse on a regular basis.

"Sorry Mom," I said as I ran up the stairs to change my clothes and grab my fencing gear.

Skirt, shirt and tie went into the laundry pile. I pulled leggings over my tights and added a baggy t-shirt. Then I pulled my sword case out from under my bed. Snapping open the latches, I raised the lid and took a moment to admire my beloved sword. I had been so glad when I'd graduated from foil to epee. The foil was such a finicky weapon, and all those judges watching made me nervous. Nervous enough to make dumb mistakes. But switching to the heavier epee, with only one judge to monitor the combats, made all the difference. Gone were the dumb mistakes. My fencing coach had been thrilled to see me excel with the epee where I'd been struggling with the foil.

I shut the lid and charged back down the stairs, trying to juggle my sword case, gym bag, and top hat, while putting on my jacket at the same time. It was a minor miracle that I didn't fall and break my neck, but by the time I reached the bottom of the stairs, everything was where it was supposed to be, hat on head, coat on back, case in hand, gym bag slung over my shoulder.

"Be back later!"

"Tom, drive your sister!" Dad yelled from his office.

"Yeah, yeah," Tommy answered, already heading out the door, car keys in hand.

Chapter Three

The Last Happy Ending I Have For A Long Time

Tommy's car was a beat up old Toyota that had many more miles behind it than it had left ahead, but somehow my brother was always able to coax it to life, get where he needed to go, and most importantly, get it to stop when he had to stop. That one time his brakes had failed and we'd sailed right through a red light had been a fluke. Good thing that there hadn't been any traffic. Tommy swore the car would always protect him, but he'd had the brakes fixed, just to be sure.

The pair of us piled into the car and after a few tense seconds of the engine whining like a certain bratty little sister not wanting to get out of bed, it sputtered awake and we were off. When we got there, I said, "Pick me up in two hours, okay?" but Tommy drove off without answering. It was the longest conversation we'd had all week.

I took my fencing lessons down at the civic centre, a big yellow brick building with glass double doors. There were halls in the centre that an organization could rent, including the training room in the basement where my fencing class was held. One wall was entirely mirrored floor to ceiling and wall to wall, doubling a ballet bar placed at waist height. Exercise mats were piled high in one corner. Windows opposite the mirrors were evenly spaced and sometimes curtained, but not that night.

Smiling greetings to my fellow fencing enthusiasts, I went into the changing room and hung up my coat and hat. I changed into the white jogging pants and white shirt I knew would be greyed with sweat by the end of the lesson. They were the only white clothing I owned, and I lamented we couldn't wear black. I found myself a set of protective padding. I hoped to get a properly fitted padded tunic of my own for Christmas, but until then I'd have to make do with whatever leftover equipment the fencing club had available. I pulled my face guard and my thick white gloves out of my gym bag and carried my sword case back into the training room.

We warmed up with some stretches, then practised advances, retreats and lunges for a few minutes, attacking our mirror doubles. I amused myself by imagining I was just slightly faster than my double. Once our instructor, Raoul, decided we were sufficiently warmed up, we paired up and put on our fencing helmets, the wire mesh faces making strangers of us all.

I was the only student to have advanced from foil to epee, so I had to fence Raoul, something I did not mind at all.

"Ready?" Raoul asked. He was tall, broad-shouldered, and lean, with curly brown hair and deep brown eyes, but the fencing mask made him the same faceless opponent as everyone else in the room, the padded tunic adding girth I knew was an illusion. I'd seen Raoul with his shirt off once, coming out of the men's changing room. Muscles cut from marble had nothing on Raoul's exceptional bod. I suspected I might have a tiny crush on my instructor. Okay, I knew I did, but he was twice my age and married, so I also knew nothing could ever happen. A girl could dream, though.

"En garde," I answered, saluting him with my epee.

We took up our positions to the shuffle of feet around us and the occasional clatter of foil on foil as my fellow students tested each other's defences. I felt all the others fade away around me, my entire world focusing on Raoul, on the tiny, almost microscopic movements of his hands, his feet. The slight raise of his shoulders. The scrape of his epee against mine. The flex of his calves as he raised himself on the balls of his feet to attack!

I narrowly parried his attack and riposted with my own. Our epees clattered against each other, almost too fast to see, attack parry riposte, back and forth for three very intense seconds. We disengaged, each retreating to en garde.

"Good," Raoul said. "Very good."

"Thanks," I answered, then launched an attack of my own.

Raoul, of course, was expecting it. He easily parried and said, "You're still telegraphing your attacks, Val."

"Tell me how to stop and I will," I answered, deflecting his riposte.

"It's your elbow," he said, catching my foible with his forte and circling his blade around and around mine, an envelopment manoeuvre I hadn't yet mastered.

He had the upper hand but I wasn't about to let him make a touch, or worse, disarm me. I advanced, sliding my blade along his until I forced him to retreat a couple of steps. He engaged me, blade to blade. Desperate, I tried the prise de fer, which was a kind of half-circle to the envelopment's fully circular manoeuvre. Raoul countered with a prise de fer of his own.

I lunged again, advancing on him. His easy deflections of my attacks made me furious, something I knew always led to his gaining a touch on me, something I also hadn't quite mastered. Raoul stepped back, retreating from my attacks, using his much longer reach to his greatest advantage.

I stopped advancing suddenly, and retreated, forcing Raoul to come forward to maintain engagement, and that's when I lunged, using the envelopment against him, putting so much force into the move that I actually succeeded in disarming him.

Raoul's epee bounced on the padded floor as the other students suddenly stopped their own fencing. Several looked as though they'd stopped long before, in order to watch the duel between us.

"Very good, Valerie," Raoul said, bowing his head in acknowledgement.

I saluted him with my epee, panting behind the grin that sprouted on my face, so proud I wanted to explode. No one could see it, of course, not behind the wire mesh of my fencing mask, but I didn't care. The grin, and the win, were mine.

Chapter Four

Things Get Epic Weird

After the lesson was over and we'd changed back to our normal clothes, I stepped outside to wait for Tommy. Moving through the clouds of cigarette smoke the few smokers in the class were making at the entrance, I stepped out into the parking lot and glanced around. No sign of Tommy. What a surprise.

"Good class," Raoul said to the smokers as he left, last. I turned at the sound of his voice.

"Good class," he repeated to me as he walked past.

"Yeah thanks," I answered, trying very hard to sound totally cool, and probably not succeeding very well. "You too."

He turned to face me, slowing to walk backwards toward his car. "You okay? Got a lift?"

"Oh. Yeah," I shrugged. I glanced around the rapidly emptying parking lot. Still no sign of Tommy.

"Okay," Raoul said, looking down to unlock his car door. "Keep practising. Mind your elbow." Door unlocked, he looked over at me and smiled. "Who knows? By next summer I might have me a new assistant."

You know when they write 'She blinked in in surprise' in books? It actually happens. I blinked in surprise. "Me?"

"You're good, Val. Very good. Pretty soon there won't be much more I can teach you."

"Oh," I said, somehow thrilled and disappointed at the same time. I hooked a thumb back over my shoulder, back toward the classroom. "I just got lucky with that disarm."

"Nope," he answered. "G'night."

"Night."

He drove off. I watched the smokers finish their cigarettes and conversations, get in their own cars and leave. I smiled and nodded good nights to them all.

Finally I was alone in the parking lot. I pulled out my cell phone to check my messages. No messages and no texts. I texted my idiot brother to see if he was on his idiot way, but there was no answering text.

The night was bright and quiet, the way autumn nights can be. Lacking the buzz and rustle of summertime insects and animals, the only sounds that I could hear were the wind in the few golden red leaves that remained, the distant hiss of traffic on the highway a couple of miles away, my own breathing (it was that quiet), and the electric hum of the solitary light that lit the parking lot.

I didn't want to get my idiot brother into trouble but he was nearly twenty minutes late. If he wasn't answering my texts then he wouldn't be likely to answer my call. I'd have to call home.

The light's electric hum grew suddenly louder. Much louder. I turned to stare at it in confusion, then jumped back, startled, as the light suddenly began sparking. Electric sparks turned to arcs of electricity, dancing blue-white from the light to the concrete sidewalk beneath. I shaded my eyes with one hand, amazed and spellbound. It seemed longer but must have only been a few seconds when the electricity stopped.

Then a chain fell from the light. Even from where I stood safely half the parking lot away, I could see that the chain ended in a handle.

Curiosity got the better of me. Not smart. The chain dangled, as near as I could tell, right from the light itself. Not from the light post, but right through the plexiglass encasing that surrounded the light bulb. I stepped toward the chain to get a better look.

It looked like a disappointingly normal chain, about the same size and thickness as one of those heavy-duty dog leashes. The metal of the chain was yellowy brownish.

"Is it brass?" I asked no one in particular. I don't usually talk to myself but sometimes it slips out, you know? As I got closer, I could see I was right. The chain was made of brass. The handle mounting was also made of brass; the handle itself was carved from some dark wood. It hung from the light to about waist-height on me.

"Wow," I admired, leaning down and poking the handle to watch it sway.

I straightened and looked around the empty parking lot, expecting someone to jump out and yell, "You been punked!" It had to be some kind of prank. Brass chains with wooden handles didn't just materialize from street lights.

I followed the chain to its end, staring into the street light until retinal spots blinded me. I blinked the spots away, then reached for the handle and gave it a yank.

Nothing happened. The chain might as well have been mounted into steel plate instead of cheap frosted plexiglass. I put down my gym bag and sword case and grabbed it with both hands.

This time I gave it a good hard yank with all my strength, and was rewarded with feeling something high above me give, just slightly. I glanced up, grinning.

Sparks exploded out of the light above me, and I gave a little yelp. It absolutely was not a shriek. Anyway, you have sparks of electricity rain down on you, and we'll see what kind of noise you make. I tried to run away, but electricity arced down all around me, in every direction, trapping me. I tried to shield myself from the killing blue-white light, but for some reason I couldn't let go of the chain. It was like my hands were glued to the wood. I shook them, trying to free them from the handle, but nothing would give. I even hiked my foot onto the handle and pushed, but felt the skin on my palms start to tear.

I had just enough time to notice that my struggles had knocked my top hat off my head when the chain began to retract into the sparking light. I quickly found myself with my arms above my head. Then my feet left the ground.

"Help!" I screamed, feeling stupid. How dumb do you have to be to fall for something like this? God, Monica was never going to let me forget it. That is, if I survived.

The chain retracted even faster, the electricity sparked even brighter, I rose even higher, and then everything went white.

Chapter Five

Mad Scientists Make Me Crazy

"Are you quite well? Can you understand me?"

I had been drunk once before in my life. Last New Year's Eve, I sneaked some of my parents' rum into my Cokes at the family's annual party. I felt really good at first, and everything was funny. Soon, though, the world moved even when I tried really hard to keep still, even when I lay down on the bathroom floor because the tiles were cold and that felt really nice against my spinning head.

This was a little like that. Everything was spinning and nothing made a lot of sense and I definitely had the urge to puke. I wasn't in a parking lot waiting for my idiot, no-good, always late brother. I wasn't lying on the concrete sidewalk under a sparking street light, which I admit hadn't been my brightest idea.

I couldn't even focus my eyes very well. Everything had a blurriness around the edges. Not that being able to see clearly would have helped.

A thin man stood near me, wearing a CD in front of his face, covering one eye like a pirate's eye patch. Light from above glared off the CD into my eyes, making me blink. He wore a crisp white shirt. A part of my brain wondered if he a paramedic? He sounded kind of British, though. What would a British paramedic be doing in the civic centre's parking lot?

"How many fingers do you see?" he asked, though it sounded more like "Hehw menny fingahs juicy?" He held up three fingers.

"All of them," I answered.

"You do understand me then?" It sounded like, 'yadu ondastond meh thin?' Look, I'll spare you any more attempts at explaining his accent. It was not-quite-British.

"Sort of? Where am I?"

"Unexpected side effect of the transference, I'm afraid." The man leaned back out of the light, disappearing into shadow.

I blinked away the blur and glanced around me. I was in a large room, much longer than it was wide, with metal walls and a metal grate floor, filled with odd machines and even odder equipment. Electricity arced between two wavy metal strips that ran the length of the room, high overhead. Occasionally the electricity would stab down to light up the glass balls that sat on top of one or another of the machines. I tried to sit up but had to settle for rolling on my side. I felt as weak as when I'd had stomach flu for over a week. In the distance, the man was turning knobs and cranking cranks, checking what looked to be glass-domed pressure gauges.

I shook my head to clear it. "Who are you?"

"Of course! Do forgive me." The man came back from the equipment he'd been checking and removed the thick rubberised leather gloves he had on, offering me his hand to shake. "Allow me to introduce myself. I am Doctor Montgomery Sweetwater, and you," he grinned with obvious pride, "you are the world's first aethernaut."

I took his hand and shook it briefly. It was hot and sweaty from being in the glove. "I'm a wha?"

He politely ignored me as I wiped my hand on my pants leg. "Aethernaut. A word of my own devising. It means, traveller from the aether."

"What's the ay-ther?"

"How much does your world know about alternate worlds?"

"Like, in sci-fi?"

"I beg your pardon?"

"Alternate realities is like, from movies and science fiction."

"Science... fiction? But science is not fictional." He seemed offended at the very thought.

"Can you shine that thing somewhere else? Bit headachy here."

He removed the CD thing he wore, messing up his thinning grey hair. I realized that the CD was a doctor's reflector. Dr. Sweetwater turned and threw a switch on the wall, and the globes on the top of the machines brightened, casting away the shadows. I blinked and winced at the light, raising a hand to shade my eyes.

"Yeah, that's much better," I grumped. I knew I was being grumpy, but I figure you'll forgive me because I'd just been kidnapped by some kind of freaky mad scientist.

He turned to me, but by the expression on his face he was clearly lost in thought. "Imagine if you will a glass of milk, in which float an infinite number of pearls."

"Pretty big glass." When I'm grumpy, I get sarcastic. Okay, I'm sarcastic a lot of the time. Anyhow.

"Indeed. Infinitely large, larger even than our own universe."

"And each of the pearls is a universe?"

That surprised the doctor, who wasn't that old, I realized, probably less than forty. "Why, yes. You have heard of alternate worlds, then?"

"Only in like, a hundred thousand movies and books." I struggled to sit properly. He helped prop me up.

"Moo-vees?"

"So I'm in an alternate reality, is what you're saying?"

"Well... yes."

"Then how come you're talking English?"

"I beg your pardon?"

I sighed, then said, very slowly, "How. Come. You. Talk. English."

"But we are not. We are speaking the King's Anglic, in which, despite your horrible accent, you seem to be quite proficient. What an amazing discovery!"

"Anglic?" I pushed myself off the table and steadied myself with both hands on the table. I could stand. Good.

"From the country of Anglica."

"Right."

This close, I could see he had bright, icy blue eyes, and his hairline had definitely started to recede. He was taller than I was, but not by much more than six inches or so (which made him not that tall for a guy, on account of, you know, I'm not that tall for a girl), and he was thin to the point of gauntness. His white smock ended at his knees; beneath that were dark blue pants and dark brown calf-high leather boots with thick rubber soles. There was featureless ring on his right middle finger made of some dark grey metal.

I gave him a good hard shove and ran for the door at the end of the room. "Nice try, jerk!"

The 'doctor' stumbled back, falling against some of his machinery. My legs weren't quite doing what I told them, but I managed to cross the room without falling down. I turned the door handle, but the door wouldn't budge.

"Miss, please, you must calm yourself," my kidnapper said, hands out, trying to calm me down. Yeah, right.

"Listen, you got the whole mad scientist thing down perfect." I worked the door to get it to open, all the while keeping an eye on him coming up behind me. "But I'm not just going to let you kill me and play with my gooey innards, you sick freak."

"Mad? Kill you?" he looked stunned and confused. "You... you mustn't call me mad. I admit some of my theories are unconventional, but... Some of my classmates called me mad, you understand."

"And now I am, jerk."

"Please. Miss. I understand this is difficult to accept."

"You're damn right it's difficult!"

The door opened behind me, finally, and I turned to run, but slammed straight into a nightmare.

"Is everything all right, Father?" the nightmare asked. "I heard shouting."

I was stunned into staring. Not polite, I know. Whatever. The nightmare looked like a tall girl with some of the worst scars I'd ever seen, criss-crossing her face and what little I could see of her hands, arms and chest. She had ragged black hair pulled back in a low, loose ponytail, and different coloured eyes. One was deep, bright blue, while the other, encircled by scar tissue, was so dark a brown it seemed nearly black. Her scars were an unhealthy yellowish colour, especially where the many stitch marks puckered her skin into a patchwork quilt.

The nightmare girl's clothes were purely functional: a greenish shirt that was a bit too small for her and a long black patched skirt that was still somehow too short for her even longer legs. Like the doctor, she also wore heavy leather boots with thick rubber soles.

Stunned, I leaned toward the girl, angling myself this way and that to get a better look at her. "That is the best make-up I've ever seen," I said, my brain retreating from uncomfortable obvious truth to manageable fiction. "Wow, seriously. Did you do it yourself?"

The scarred girl shied away from my inspection, raising a hand to shield her face. "Please. Don't."

"Everything's fine, my dear," the doctor said to the girl. "Please return to your duties."

"Yes, Father."

That's when my brain said, *Hey stupid, get moving!* I shoved past the scarred girl and ran out of the room. The next chamber was a kind of library, or study. A pair of elegant leather armchairs sat facing one another. Brass nails trimmed the arms of the chair, and lace handkerchiefs were placed over the headrests. A small round table with beautifully carved legs sat between the two armchairs. On the table sat a cup of tea and an open book, a pencil marking the unknown reader's place. Dark wood bookcases stacked deep with leather-bound books lined every wall, and what looked like gas lamps sprouted wherever there wasn't a bookcase. But they couldn't be gas lamps, since the bright white light they gave off was definitely electrical in nature. Gas light would be yellower.

I absorbed it all in an instant, my mind noticing details without cataloguing them. The only thing that really registered was the door opposite me, made of rich dark wood, with a brass handle.

"Stop her, my dear!" Dr. Sweetwater ordered.

The scarred girl tried to grab me and nearly did, getting two surprisingly powerful handfuls of my coat. I shrugged it off and ran for the door. How could I abandon my beloved coat, you ask? Simple, when your choice is your coat or your own skin.

"Please, stop," the girl called after me. They were both so creepily polite!

"Yeah right." I opened the door.

Chapter Six

Out of a Nightmare and Into a Hurricane

Frigid air blasted through the open door, carrying in sheets of rain. It was a storm the likes of which I had only ever seen in Youtube footage or horror movies, of which I am not a fan. Crazy freezing cold water falling, not in pleasant drops, but in huge angry slaps of rain. I was soaked in a second as I left the warmth and light of the elegant sitting room for the frenzied frightening freedom of the night outside. When I get freaked out I alliterate a lot, be warned.

Two steps told me more than I ever wanted to know. Two steps was the furthest I could get in a straight line away from the door, which opened onto a metal grate balcony with wooden handrails.

"Please Miss, come back inside," the scarred girl said calmly. "You'll catch your death."

"I promise to explain everything," the mad doctor added. "Please!"

"Get away from me!"

The balcony curved around the left side of the outside of the room, so I ran back that way. The wind picked up, slamming me into the metallic wall, and the balcony flooring lurched suddenly. Lightning split the sky in the distance, and that's when I realized we were high in the air. I grabbed the polished handrail with fingers that had suddenly knuckled white and looked down.

Way down.

We were somewhere over an ocean, or at least that's what I assumed the rolling, heaving, sickening blanket of silvery blackness was, far beneath us. Lightning arced across the sky again, and thunder cracked hard on its heels. Despite myself, I ducked.

"That's not going to help much," the doctor called out. He'd found a set of brass goggles from somewhere, giving him an even more sinister look. "Ducking, I mean."

"Whatever!" I couldn't see behind him, but I had a feeling the scarred girl wasn't with him. I turned and ran along the balcony, trying to keep from slipping to my watery death. Not that I'd survive the fall, I guess. The doctor hurried along after me, pleading with me to come back. I risked a glance up, and saw by the flash of lightning illumination that the balcony lay under a huge oval balloon.

"This is unbelievable," I said to myself. "Monica's going to freak. Kidnapped by a mad scientist in a blimp!"

I spotted a ladder about halfway down the length of the blimp and ran for it. I wasn't sure what good it would do, but I'd be damned if I was going to let Doctor Psycho kill me that easy. How we got over an ocean would be something to deal with later, assuming I survived the climb, the storm, and the scarred girl running straight at me.

I stopped short so suddenly I lost my footing on the rain-slicked metal grating. I fell clumsily and skidded right past the scarred girl, who had such a funny look of amazement on her goggled face that I surprised myself by actually laughing out loud as I passed her. My backside as sore as if I'd slid down a cheese grater, I hauled myself to my feet and grabbed the ladder rungs.

"Please! Stop!" the scarred girl yelled over the storm.

"They sure are polite homicidal maniacs," I said to myself as I hurried up the ladder.

Climbing a metal ladder in a lightning storm probably wasn't the brightest thing that I had ever done, but then I consoled myself with the thought that since we were flying, there was zero chance I was grounded. At least, that's how I hoped it worked.

I climbed the ladder, rain lashing against me pitilessly. Lightning and thunder pounded my eyes and ears, so bright and so loud I thought for a second I would pass out, total sensory overload, so I clung desperately to the rungs of the ladder.

"Miss!" the scarred girl yelled, grabbing at my foot. She'd climbed up after me. Talk about dedication! "Please, you'll get yourself killed!"

I kicked at her hand to loosen her grip. "Let go of me!"

But the scarred girl was incredibly strong, holding onto my booted foot with a vice-like grip. "Just come down, miss, please!"

"You want me to come down?" I asked under my breath. "Fine!" I shouted, then jumped off the rung, landing hard with both feet on the scarred girl's face, and grabbing a rung before I fell the whole way. Not a half-bad move, even if it nearly tore my arm off at the shoulder. The scarred girl fell to the balcony floor, stunned senseless.

I climbed for my life. Up the ladder, at least thirty feet or so, to the roof of the blimp's cabin. Overhead, the blimp's balloon hung fat and swollen, blotting out everything. It was so close, if I had reached for it, I could have touched it, but staying on the blimp's roof was taking all my strength and attention. The wind, squeezed between the balloon and the cabin, blew even harder than it had been on the balcony. It forced me to my hands and knees to keep from falling off. Plummeting to my death in the roiling, rolling ocean far far beneath me seemed imminent. I had to fight a sudden urge to vomit.

I crawled along the rain-slicked metal roof, desperately trying to keep from falling off. I was concentrating so hard on staying alive that I didn't hear the clank of a hatch opening behind me, didn't sense the doctor closing in on me, didn't realize anyone else was on the roof with me until it was too late. A gloved hand grabbed my face from behind, a foul-smelling cloth covered my mouth and nose, and then, blackness.

Chapter Seven

Weirdest. Geography Lesson. EVER.

My first thought when I woke up was that I must have fallen off my bed and slept right through it, otherwise, why would I be sleeping on the floor?

I opened my eyes, expecting to see my bookcase filled with anime and books that was next to my bed. Instead, I saw a blank metal wall. I looked around. I was on a table.

The same metal table I'd been on before.

It all came back. The mad scientist, the scarred girl, the blimp.

All of it.

The manacles around my wrists were new, though. I pulled at them, tugging the thick metal chain that bound them, and me, to the table. They gave a depressingly heavy rattle as I did, utterly ruining any chance of escaping that I might have had.

My soaking wet clothes were gone. Instead, I wore a shirt that was way too big for me, the sleeves rolled up at the cuff, and a pair of way too big for me pants, the legs also rolled up. I guessed I looked like a little kid, dressed up in her dad's clothes.

"Ah, you're awake," the doctor said in his weirdly not-quite-British accent.

I sighed and rolled over, glaring at my captor. "Okay, psycho, get it over with. Kill me."

The doctor looked shocked. "Kill you? Dear heavens, no! I would sooner kill myself!"

"Deal!" I said. "You go do that, then."

The doctor smiled an indulgent smile at me, which only made me angry. I hate being patronized. He moved toward me slowly and calmly, hands clasped in front of him.

"No my dear, none of us will be dying very soon. I am very sorry about all this. I should have explained myself a little better. You see.."

But I wasn't listening. As the doctor moved toward me, I could see past him to the scarred girl behind him, lying on another table that leaned at an angle against the laboratory's metal wall. Thick leather bands kept the scarred girl from sliding to the floor. The electricity arcing overhead made a grisly strobe effect on the scarred girl's face. Raw wet muscles and bones were visible under the split skin... but no blood spilled from the wound.

"Oh man," I said, as the urge to vomit came back. I couldn't tear my eyes away from the scarred girl. "Is she dead?" I asked.

"Eve is quite resilient to injury," the doctor said proudly. "Like all patchworks."

"Patchworks?"

"Beings sewn together from the remainders of others. Quite difficult to build, as you might imagine." The doctor went to the girl and pulled her head forward, brushing her shaggy ponytail off of her neck.

I saw something metallic glint off the back of her neck. The doctor pulled down a thick cable sheathed in rubber, attaching the brass fitting on the end to the metallic knob sticking out of the girl's spine.

"But ultimately worth the investment," the doctor said as he stepped away from the girl. He followed the cable to a large machine, lowered his goggles and threw the switch.

The lights dimmed and electricity arced all over the girl. Her skeleton glowed briefly through her skin and she jerked and danced on table. The thick leather bands held fast, though they quickly began to smoulder.

"God, stop!" I shouted over the electrical crackle.

Okay, I know what you're going to say. Total Frankenstein, right? Let me tell you something. Watching something in a movie is nothing compared to seeing it happen in real life. Frankenstein was actually the last thing on my mind at the moment. Mostly I was thinking, *OH GOD OH GOD MAKE IT STOP PLEASE GOD MAKE IT STOP!*

The doctor released the switch and turned off the machine. Eve jerked about a little longer, then threw her head back and screamed. Her eyes blinked open, and she looked around the room, terrified for a brief moment, then visibly relaxed.

"Do forgive my outburst," she apologized, as though she hadn't just been electrocuted back to life.

"Not at all, dear heart," the doctor soothed as he undid the leather bands. "Perfectly understandable."

"Thank you, Father," Eve said as she stepped off the table.

"You sustained a bit of an injury, my dear," the doctor said. "You'll want to see to it."

"Yes Father," she said, one scarred hand reached up to feel at the open, gaping, bloodless wound. She turned away, embarrassed.

The doctor turned back to me. The flickering electrical lighting gave his face a very sinister look. As if this whole situation needed to get more sinister.

"Now then. I apologize for the manacles but we simply cannot allow you to come to any harm." He smiled in what he probably thought was a charming way. "You're too important, my dear."

"Suuuuuure I am."

"I understand you may be sceptical, but it remains the truth. You are the first aethernaut in our history. And I, I am responsible for your presence on our world."

"Wow. That's incredible. Way to go. Can I leave now?"

"Leave? Dear me, no. There's so much to learn!"

I frowned, pinching the bridge of my nose with one manacled hand. "Okay, so, wait. Let me see if I've got this straight. You made a machine that, what? Brought me here from my world?"

"Correct."

"And this is an alternate world?"

"Also correct."

"Where people speak perfect English."

"Anglic is the language of Anglica, an island in the Northern Sea. It is one of many languages the people of this world speak. Most speak Atlan, however." He sniffed distastefully. "I choose to speak the language of the land of my birth, rather than that of the governing class. Another reason I was mocked at the academy."

"Okay, so forget that. If this is another world, what year is it?"

"By the ancient reckoning, it is the year 6897."

My voice rose an octave. "Six thousand?!"

"Dated from the founding of Atlan."

"Okay, that's twice. What's Atlan?"

The doctor's distaste was obvious from his expression. "Atlan is a place, a continent to the west of Europa."

"That's America," I said.

"America?"

"Okay, next thing you're going to tell me there's no America."

The doctor looked confused for a second, then his expression settled on curious excitement, or excited curiosity. Like I was an especially challenging problem he wanted to solve, and he really loved solving problems.

"If you give me your word you'll not try to escape, I'll free you from those manacles, and we can retire to a more hospitable setting for tea and genteel conversation." He smiled again. It wasn't a nice smile, but I got the feeling he honestly didn't intend to feast on my gooey innards, at least. Or do worse stuff, either. I decided to trust him, since I didn't really have a lot of options and anyway the manacles were starting to chafe.

"Okay," I answered, holding out my hands for him to unlock them.

Instead, he went to another one of his machines and threw a switch.

Electricity arced along the chains. I thought for a second he had changed his mind and was frying me to be done with me and my constant questions, but when the electricity touched my skin it just barely tingled, like suddenly getting pins-and-needles that disappeared instantaneously. Highly weird. Even weirder, the manacles popped open.

"Shall we?" he asked, hands outstretched ahead of him, ushering me into that sitting room I'd nearly escaped through.

When I stepped through the door Eve was just finishing sewing her face shut. Watching wasn't pleasant, seeing her use tiny scissors to snip the thick black thread, but at least there was no blood and she genuinely didn't seem fussed that I'd given her a new scar.

"Excellent, my dear," the doctor said as he inspected her stitches. "We shall make a first-rate assistant of you yet."

Eve smiled shyly, ducking her chin and looking away. I got the feeling she'd be blushing if her blood flowed normally, which it obviously didn't.

"Now, would you be so good as to provide us with tea while we converse?" Dr. Sweetwater asked her.

She jumped up from the low stool she was sitting on. "Of course, Father," she said, then left the sitting room through a third door I hadn't noticed in my last exploration of the room. Of course, I was running for my life at the time, so I don't feel too bad about that particular oversight. Besides, it was right next to the door to the lab, behind me.

"Please, my dear, be seated," the doctor said. I chose one of the leather armchairs at random and sat down.

He looked at me with those piercing eyes of his and asked, "Do you know, in all our earlier excitement, I believe we neglected to properly introduce ourselves? Doctor Montgomery Sweetwater, at your service."

"Yeah, I remember."

"And you are?"

"Oh." For some reason, I still didn't quite trust him. Being kidnapped from my home planet tends to make me distrustful, I guess. I didn't want to give him my real name. My mind danced around, looking for a reasonable alias. "I'm... Sunset. Val. Sunset Val."

It killed me to use the nickname my uncle had given me, but my mouth acted before my brain thought it out completely.

The doc looked confused. "I see. And which is your given name and which your patronymic?"

"Huh?"

"Do your people practice the custom of continuing a familial designation through generations?"

"Oh! Yeah, sure. It's uh. Sorta both?"

"Sunset Val, I welcome you on behalf of all inhabitants of this planet, Ayrth."

He looked at me, obviously expecting some kind of reply. "Um. Thanks? So uh, you were going to explain Atlan?"

"Of course," he said. "But perhaps it would be easier for me to show you."

"Okay."

He stood and went to the bookshelves that lined the wall to our left. Well, his right, my left. Anyway. He pulled on one of the books and the shelves swung away from the wall on their own, folding in on themselves. They revealed an incredibly detailed map of the world, twice as long as I could reach with both arms outstretched, and nearly as high as I was tall.

Europe was right there, pretty much the same as I remembered it, with Africa beneath and Asia sprawling off to the side. Australia was all tucked away in the corner as usual, with the same scattering of islands through the Pacific. A few more islands than I remembered there being in the Indian Ocean, but otherwise pretty normal, as far as I could remember from geography class.

Where things really got weird was in the Americas.

The ice cream cone shape of South America lay at a thirty-degree angle into the Pacific, and it wasn't connected to North America at all. North America was barely recognizable. Everything from the Mississippi to the East Coast, including a big chunk of Canada's Atlantic seaboard, was separated from the rest of the continent, floating in the middle of what I knew was the Atlantic Ocean. The rest of North America seemed to be pretty much the same, except for a huge semi-circular coastline right through where Nebraska, Iowa and Kansas would have been. Basically, the Gulf of Mexico was where the American Mid-west should have been. What had been the East Coast of the United States was labelled "Atlan". Roughly where Manhattan should have been was a city named Neptopolis.

"Atlan," the doc said, not bothering to hide the bitterness in his voice.

I turned to face him, though I couldn't remember when I'd stood and gone to the map. Geography had never been my most favourite class, but I'd gotten good enough grades to keep me on the Honour roll. The map was incredible, a work of art.

"The seat of all worldly power," he said. "The crown jewel of the Empire. Centre of art, literature, science, and even magic. Though I might aside that magic is simply misunderstood science, waiting to be properly researched and explained. Once the sciences of chemistry and medicine were the province of mages and alchemists, thought of as witchcraft, but science will out! One day all will be understood by science, and what a glorious day that will be!"

"I hate to interrupt a good monologue, Doc." Because I could tell he was just getting started and it didn't have much to do with me. Or so I thought at the time. "But getting back to Atlan?"

"Of course, of course," he said.

Eve brought in tea and served us each a cup. I'd never been much of a tea drinker. Give me a triple-espresso latte any day. But I hadn't had anything to eat or drink since I'd arrived, so I took my cup with three sugars and cream. The doc had his with lemon, and Eve poured herself a cup with one sugar. Out of the corner of my eye, when the doc wasn't looking, I saw Eve sneak a second lump of sugar into her tea. There was hope for her yet.

"Atlan conquered Europa some four thousand years ago," the doc explained, sipping his tea. "From there the Afric continent was a logical step, and then the Zhou."

I waved a hand at what would have been North and South America back home. "What about these two continents?"

He raised his cup, pointing at the northern continent. "The Confederacy of the Thousand Tribes made treaties with the Atlan invaders. Treaties of peace, enforced by their mastery of what the superstitious would call spirit magic. No Atlan army has ever managed to defeat the Confederacy on their home lands, though many have tried over the millennia."

"And the southern continent?" I checked the name written on the map. "Amazonia?"

A shadow of sadness passed over his face. "Those heathens have also managed to thwart invasion, by far more brutal means."

"But surely the Atlan forces have better technology?" I twirled a finger around, to indicate the blimp and everything else that surrounded us.

"Superior technology can only go so far," the doc said. "The Amazonian peoples fight with a blood fury, terrible to behold. And every man, woman and child fights, heedless of their own safety. Once the Atlan forces might have subdued them, long ago, but as each invasion was defeated, the Amazonians would capture weapons and technologies, learning from their captives, making their own improvements. They are every bit as intelligent and advanced as we are now, sad to say."

"So Atlan controls Europa, Zhou, and Afric? What about here?" I pointed to Australia, which had no name written across it.

"No one controls that place," the doc said. He seemed shocked at the very idea. "It is a sun-blasted scrub land, filled with poisonous flora and fauna, and an incomprehensible native population that seem to exist and not exist at the same time. The laws of science and nature have no place there, twisted and perverted beyond reason. It is a land of madness."

"Okay, so no vacations Down Under, gotcha."

"Your words seem so similar to our own, and then at times, so strange. Fascinating."

"Thanks?"

"No, thank you," the doc said. "Your very existence will assure my place in the annals of scientific history."

"Glad to help," I said with a grin. Why not? It looked like I was going to be famous. On another Earth, true, but so what? "So how about we talk about getting me home?"

"All in good time, my dear," he said. Then the lights all turned bright red.

An alarm sounded, deafening in intensity. I clapped my hands over my ears. Eve jumped up and went through the third door, the doc right on her heels. I followed them, hoping to get away from that shrieking alarm.

Chapter Eight

Out of the Frying Pan, Into the Flier

I should have stayed in the sitting room.

For one thing, there was a lot more space. The third door opened on a very narrow hallway, not even as wide as my two arms outstretched, panelled in dark wood and carpeted with a worn red carpet. The carpet had yellow lightning bolts embroidered along the length. There were a couple of portraits, and some framed black and white (or I should say, dark brown and creamish) pictures hung along the inner wall, the wall that ran the length of the lab. The outer wall had one single window, shuttered against the storm. All in all, it was pretty claustrophobic.

We came to a couple of doors that opened off the inner wall, which we passed right by. One was obviously a galley kitchen. The other branched off into another hallway. I didn't stop for a closer look, but a quick glance showed me three other doors in that hall, all opening in the direction we were heading.

Which wasn't very far, either, because we came to yet another door, which the doc threw open. This door was metal and riveted along its edges. It opened with a spoked wheel instead of a proper door knob. We stepped through the doorway into what was very obviously the blimp's control room. It was tiny, barely able to hold the three of us. As it was I had to stay standing in the doorway. There were control panels on every available surface, filled with switches and knobs and gauges. The far wall was entirely made of small panels of glass, showing us the storm raging outside. Eve dropped into the only seat in the room, slipping her arms through two shoulder straps.

"What's going on?" I yelled over the shrieking alarm. Of course, that's exactly when Eve threw a switch on a panel, turning off the alarm. So I wound up yelling at the top of my lungs for no reason. Thanks, Eve.

"That was our proximity alarm," the doc explained. His hands flew across the control panel, throwing switches, tapping gauges. He leaned over to get a better look at something on a very tiny glowing panel, sort of like a round television screen about the size of my palm. Lit from below by the greenish-white light, the doc looked every bit as sinister as I thought he was when I first woke up on that table. "There is a ship off our port side, coming along."

"Not friends, then?"

"No, not friends." The doc looked up, out the window. He wasn't looking at the storm. His face was very bleak "Pirates."

"Pirates?!"

"Eve, evasive manoeuvres."

"Right away, Father."

Doc glanced at me. "I do apologize, my dear. This wasn't exactly the reception I was hoping for you."

"Oh, no big," I answered, waving it off. "I deal with pirates all the time."

"You do?"

"No."

He frowned at my joke and turned back to his control panel. Hey, a little levity to lighten a dark moment never hurt, right?

I felt the entire blimp shudder as Eve kicked it into high gear. Which, for a blimp, meant after about ten seconds we started to feel like we might possibly be turning to our right. It was a little tough to tell.

"What do we do?" I asked.

"We shall try outrunning them," the doc said grimly. "If that should fail, then you and Eve will escape in the ornithopter."

"Father, I won't leave you!" Eve yelled over her shoulder.

"An admirable sentiment, my dear," the doc said. "But misplaced, I fear. The orny has only two seats, and you are by far the better pilot. Sunset Val's value to science is much greater than myself."

"What's an orny?" I asked.

Doc didn't even bother to glance at me this time. All his attention was focussed on the panel in front of him. "An ornithopter," he said, as if that explained anything. "Eve, set a course to bring us above the storm, please, then ready the orny."

"As you wish, Father." Eve pulled on the stick between her legs, then cranked a wheel to her right, and flipped a bunch of switches on her left. Then she climbed out of the pilot chair and moved toward me, a grim look on her face. I stepped out of the control room into the hallway, getting out of her way.

"This way please, miss," she said, grabbing my arm and pulling me along. She was nearly a foot taller than me and outweighed me by at least forty or fifty pounds, so I pretty much let myself be dragged along.

She turned at the hallway that branched off the main one. She pushed me to one side at the middle door. "Stay here, please, miss." The politeness of her words was completely at odds with her attitude. It wasn't a request.

Eve went through the door just as the entire blimp began to shake and shudder. I guessed that we were entering the cloud cover. Or else the pirates had locked onto us and were boarding. Something bad, anyway.

I peeked through the door. It was a small, cramped quarters, basically just a bed along one wall and a desk that folded into the wall adjacent. I guessed that one of the other doors must have been Doc's quarters, too.

Eve stuffed things into a small satchel looped from one shoulder to her opposite hip. A necklace, a really ragged rag doll, a book, a photo of Doc Sweetwater in an elegant brass frame. Goggles slipped over her head to rest on her collar bone.

"Eve, listen, what's the deal?"

She glanced at me, scowling. She huffed out an angry breath. "The doctor is trying to save our lives by leading the pirates into the storm. Only the most desperate of scoundrels would follow a blimp this size into a storm."

Eve slammed the door to her quarters behind her and grabbed my hand, pulling me along. "The profits are not enough to justify the danger. Unless of course they are slavers. Regardless, should they wish to take us, they will pay dearly. Not that we have any defences or weapons, of course. The doctor is a pacifist, a man of science."

"Since when do science and peace go together?" I asked. Eve shoved me toward a ladder that was behind the third door.

"All science is dedicated to bringing universal understanding and peace to all humanity," Eve said, sounding like she was quoting someone. Probably Doc.

I climbed down the ladder. "And gunpowder is just used for fireworks, am I right?"

Eve didn't say anything to that, just went to this big shape covered with a canvas tarp. She started pulling on the canvas, and I went to help her.

Underneath was a machine. It kind of looked like one of those ultra-light planes, all tubes and gears and bolts and chains and exposed hoses and stuff, only instead of regular plane wings it had four long oval shapes jutting from the middle of the machine to the end of the tail. With the side-by-each seats up front and no canopy to speak of, it looked like a giant dragonfly built from the world's biggest Meccano set. Three thick chains ran from the body of the metal dragonfly to the girders in the ceiling overhead.

Eve jumped into one of the seats and I joined her, sitting in the other. "Wait, wait! We can't leave without the doc! He'll die if the pirates take the blimp!"

"Miss Val," she said with polite restraint. Her fingers flew across the machine's control panel in front of us, turning cranks, pulling levers, flipping switches. "The only man I have ever known to treat me with kindness and affection, my own creator, has trained me since my rebirth to obey his every command. And I will not disappoint him. Dr. Sweetwater will draw off any pursuit and elude them in the clouds of the storm. We will hopefully be beneath their notice, small as we are."

"And if he doesn't? And if we don't?"

"At worst he will be captured, tortured for information, and killed."

"What about us?!"

Eve looked at me with her different coloured eyes. Anger, resentment, fear, pain, and an infinite amount of patience pretty much radiated from them. "If we are taken, well, I hope for your sake they kill us. A slave's life in some Atlan manor is not something I would wish on a foe, much less a friend."

I almost said we weren't friends, we'd barely met, but she reached out of the cockpit and pulled a big lever, which opened the belly doors. The dragonfly fell about a foot, nearly plummeting us to our deaths. Thank god the chains held.

I strapped myself in, slipping my arms through the thick leather shoulder straps, padded with even thicker wool. The hurricane winds of the storm whipped my hair into my face. With the belly doors open we clearly heard the winds howling, like a thousand wrathful wraiths, desperate for our deaths.

I prepared myself for the end, hanging on to the straps with fingers knuckling white. I'd like to say I found religion in those moments, or that my all too short life flashed before my eyes, but neither happened. I closed my eyes and saw nothing but blackness. Well, blackness and those little patterns of light that you see when you squeeze your eyes shut too tight.

Eve had flipped another switch and the dragonfly's wings unfolded, swinging forward to lock into place with a *CTHUNK!* that would have been deafening if I wasn't already deafened by the howling winds. I glanced back at the wings. They began to move in small circles, the way insects' wings move. Now we really looked like a giant Meccano dragonfly.

There was a huge explosion somewhere to our left, one that rocked the entire blimp, and the dragonfly suddenly began listing towards the left, hanging from the chains.

I grabbed Eve's arm. "Wait!" I yelled over the wind. "How do we find the doc again?"

"We have a rendezvous point!" she yelled back. "A small island off the coast of Eire! Now hold on miss!"

"No, wait, what about the machine that brought me here?! What if the blimp is taken?!"

Eve looked at me, then shrugged. "Let us hope the blimp is not taken, then!" she yelled apologetically, then threw a switch. Electricity raced up the thick chains holding us up, and they let go of us.

We fell. I would be totally awesome if I could say I kept it together, riding it down into the stormy sea far below, but the truth is, I screamed. A lot. I've never really liked roller coasters, and the freefall is why. Not my favourite thing.

Also, hello? Pirates, a storm, drowning? Also not my favourite things. At least, not right at that moment, anyway.

The truth is, we fell for like, five seconds, then the dragonfly's wings built up enough speed or lift or whatever to hold us up, and we stopped falling.

The rain, however, hadn't, so we were soaked in seconds. Again. My soaking wet hair whipped me in the face, infinitely less pleasurable than the dry hair had been. I found myself wishing for a set of goggles, like Eve's.

"How much fuel does this, this, thing have?"

"Ornithopter," Eve said, distracted, as she whipped her head around to try and spot the blimp. "Enough to make the rendezvous point, miss."

"Is that enough to out race them?" I asked, pointing with one hand as I pushed soaking wet hair out of my eyes with the other.

She turned to see what I was pointing at. Three other ornithopters, larger than ours, sped out of the darkness, lit only by the occasional flash of lighting. Each held four people.

Eve took us into a steep dive, trying to draw them off from pursuing the blimp. Two of them continued on their path, but one broke formation and followed us down, down, down.

Imagine the most terrifying, dangerous, scariest roller coaster you've ever been on in your life. Now multiply that by oh, a million. That's pretty much what it felt like, diving toward a rolling ocean during a lightning storm in the middle of the night, riding something that looked like my stupid brother had built it when he was ten, chased by sky pirates. You're damn right I screamed again.

"Please, miss," Eve said, and I wasn't sure if she meant for me to calm down or was praying that our ornithopter would miss the waves crashing beneath us. Our orny pulled up from the steep dive just feet above the waves. Our pursuers weren't so lucky. A fifty foot wave crashed right into them as they pulled out of their dive, swatting them out of the sky as effectively as a giant with a flyswatter.

"YEAH!" I yelled in triumph, turning back to see if there were any survivors. In that stormy sea, I really doubted it. I pounded Eve's shoulder, but she was built like oak under a wet blanket. She flashed me a quick but surprisingly gorgeous smile, then began to climb higher into the air.

Right into an ambush.

Chapter Nine

Enter the Pirate, Exit the Patchwork

There were three other ornithopters in the air, hurtling down at us. Eve spun out of the way, dodging and banking, putting the orny through the worst, most amazing manoeuvres you could possibly imagine. They spun and twirled and looped around us, all the while lightning flashed and thunder rolled. Total roller coaster nightmare from hell. I was relieved that I hadn't eaten in hours, except for a few sips of tea. There was less to come out when I threw up.

We dodged the first and second orny, then the third one was on our tail for a while. Eve tried everything to shake him loose, diving and climbing, banking left and right, looping over ourselves, everything, but she couldn't lose him. He was too good. And in the few seconds we lost trying to shake him, the other two caught up to us.

"Why aren't they shooting us?!"

Eve didn't bother to look at me to answer. "We are worth more alive than dead, miss! It's clear they are slavers intent on our capture!"

"Slavers?! Slaves? We're going to be slaves?!"

"Not if I can outrun them, miss!"

There was a flash of lightning even brighter and louder than the others. I looked up.

And learned what real despair meant.

The doc's blimp plummeted past us as we watched, burning. Bright yellow-green flames coated the entire length of the blimp's deflated balloon, trailing out like a comet's tail behind the cabin as it fell.

"NO!" Eve shrieked. "FATHER!"

We were buffeted from below by the winds of the pirate orny's wings. My alliteration wasn't too terrible, so I wasn't freaking out that badly. But my only way home was on that blasted blimp, descending to its destruction. Okay, yeah, pretty freaked.

Like the blimp's balloon, all the air seemed to go out of Eve. She sat there, flying pretty much on autopilot, allowing our pirate captors to herd us where they wanted us to go.

A huge dark shape loomed up out of the darkness. Lightning flashes revealed it to be a giant blimp, much much larger than the doc's.

I couldn't tear my eyes away from the blimp above us. "Um, Eve?"

The three ornithopters were joined by a fourth, and they surrounded us. We were herded into position to enter a docking bay at the centre of the huge ship that hung under the massive balloon.

"Eve?!"

As we hovered into place, angry men stood to either side of the bay. They wore a variety of outfits, mismatched and slapdash. Tricorn hats and swallowtail coats and breeches were thrown together with trench coats and aviator caps and jodhpurs. Knee-high boots and buckled shoes and even bare feet, and every single one of them wore goggles. The lightning flashes below us silvered their lenses, giving them a sinister, almost inhuman appearance.

"EVE!"

They tossed hooked lines at our orny, catching onto struts and tubes and pipes, then they hauled us to a waiting platform. Eve shut down the engine. The whine of the wings slowed to a rumble, then stopped.

Eve unbuckled her shoulder straps and launched herself out of the orny, roaring in rage. She caught one pirate slaver on the side of his head with her huge fist and he went down like a marionette with its strings cut. Another pirate was almost as unlucky, getting a kick to the gut from Eve's thick-soled boot. It took six guys to pile on her to get her under control, and still she was going crazy.

I sat where I was. I think I must have been in shock. One of the pirates grabbed my arm, unfastened the straps, and hauled me out of the orny. Manacled my wrists. Shoved me over to where they held Eve down.

A tall, skeletally thin man all dressed in black made his way through the crowd. His long black hair was slicked back into a tight ponytail, which only made his large, pointed nose that much more prominent. His beady black eyes bore down on me.

"Speakay Anglic?" he asked.

"I hope you rot on the gallows, you murderer!" Eve answered.

Behind him, the other ornithopters were being hauled in and placed in a huge semi-circular rack that ran the entire width of the docking bay. He looked down at the still struggling Eve on the floor. Distaste clear on his face, he thumbed a switch on his walking stick. "Patchworks," he muttered , his nasal voice filled with disgust. He waved his free hand, and the pirates holding her down jumped clear. Then he jabbed Eve with his stick.

Electricity arced through her, making her rigid as all her muscles clenched.

"Stop it!" I struggled to free my arms from the burly pirates to either side of me.

Eve collapsed to the ground as he released the switch on his walking stick. She was completely unconscious.

"Well, we might get some collector or freak show who wants it," the pirate in black said in almost the same not-quite-British accent the doc and Eve had. He turned to me. When he spoke I noticed his teeth were quite crooked. "You cost me four men and an orny," he said. He took a step to tower over me, grabbing my face in his long, bony, callused fingers.

I tried to pull away. "Hey!"

"Speak when you're spoken to," he said, shaking my face roughly and squeezing. "Now. Maintain a civil acceptance of your fate and you'll not be harmed. Some slavers mistreat their slaves, whipping them, starving them, making sure they're too weak and too tired to cause any trouble, packing them in like cord wood. Not me. Not Captain Crow. That right boys?"

The other pirates paused in their work hauling the ornithopters on board and storing them in the racks to cheer their agreement.

"No, you'll find Captain Crow's a fair master," he said. "Work hard, you'll be fed well. Work soft, you won't be fed. Get me?"

I nodded, not wanting him to freak out and zap me with the stick he'd used on Eve. He shook my face, roughly.

"Get me?"

"Yes!"

"Yes, what?"

"Yes..." It took a second for me to understand. "Yes. I get you. Captain."

He grinned a crooked, not at all nice grin, then let go of my face. "Put her in with the others."

The two pirates holding me spun me around. Before they dragged me out of the hold, I heard Captain Crow announce, "Chins up boys! This wasn't all that bad! One more score and we're off to market!"

Chapter Ten

If I'd Known There Was An Exam, I Would Have Studied

They dragged me to a room. Actually, 'dragged' makes it sound like I resisted. I couldn't. I was still numb with shock. I'd been kidnapped, brought to another world, drugged, chained, chased, captured, kidnapped again and chained again, all in the space of a couple of hours. My only way home was sinking to the bottom of the ocean. The only people who knew I was from another planet were dead. Or as dead as a patchwork ever got, anyway. And besides, the two dragging me were definitely of the goonish persuasion. Big, strong, silent. Scarred and not that well acquainted with personal grooming, or even basic hygiene.

The room they tossed me in was pretty bare. Bare metal walls, riveted at regular intervals. No porthole. A second door led off to my right. It was locked. A bunk was bolted to the floor, a thin mattress lay atop it. No blanket. A quick check proved the mattress was fastened to the bunk somehow.

I sat down on the bunk. That's when I noticed the smell. It wasn't pleasant. Kind of like the bathroom floor of a gas station, all pee and motor oil. I stood up again.

The second door opened and a tall shapely blonde woman stepped in, carrying a small black leather suitcase and a bundle of grey cloth tucked under her arm. I suppose you might call her 'statuesque', which is kind of a nice way of saying she was a frickin' Amazon. She wore a dark green leather corset over a paler green blouse. Her tight black jodhpurs fit like a second skin, tucked into thick-soled black high-heeled leather boots, heavy on the buckles from ankle to knee. She had black leather gloves on.

But her clothes, while showcasing her impressive figure, weren't her most significant feature. No, that award had to go to the scar that ran from the left corner of her lip to the outer corner of her left eye, puckering her face into a permanent sneer. Her eyes were pure ice blue. Her hair was pulled back in a severe bun.

"Anglic, yes?" she asked, but not in the not-quite-British accent the doc, Eve and the Captain had. Hers was more not-quite-Russian, or not-quite-

Polish, or some other not-quite-Slavic.

I crossed my arms, or at least crossed them as much as the manacles would allow. "Yeah."

"Good. Take off your clothes."

"What?! No!"

"Take off your clothes, or I will call in the guards and they will take them off of you." She smiled, lips pressed tightly together, a fearsome sight. And she knew it. "It is less pleasant that way."

"I'll bet. Why take off my clothes?"

"You must be inspected. Medically."

"By you?"

"Of course."

"You're a doctor?"

"That is what I believe I implied."

The thought of being undressed by the two goons who'd hauled me before Doctor Bitch held little appeal, so I stripped down to my undies and bra. At least they were just my basic blacks. If they were the ones with the pink hearts my sisters got me last Valentine's Day as a joke, I think I would have died of embarrassment.

"That's where I draw the line," I told her. "More than that, you'll have to call for reinforcements."

"More is not necessary," she said, fitting her reflector over her scarred eye.

She poked. She prodded. She pinched. She checked my mouth, my eyes, my ears, my heartbeat. Did all that doctor stuff, only she apparently skipped class the day they taught 'How to treat the patient with respect and not freak them out more than they absolutely need to be freaked out.'

When she was done, she reached into her case and pulled out a small metallic rectangle about the size of my hand. I briefly contemplated what she was going to do with it when it became clear. The rectangle opened like a clam shell and she pulled out a small brown cigarillo. She lit it with a match that bloomed into sulphurous flame when struck against the wall.

She blew out smoke to extinguish the match. "You will do. Your hair, the colour. It is natural?"

I was offended that she asked and relieved that she hadn't checked to make sure on her own. "Yes."

"Good. You will fetch a good price at market. Perhaps you will be spared the pleasure houses. I do not know. It is not my decision."

"Pleasure houses don't sound too bad."

She raised her eyebrow at me, taking a drag of her cigarillo. "It is the last place a girl as pretty as you would ever want to end up. Subjected to the depravities of lust, over and over again, until you died from some disease."

Oh. That kind of pleasure house. "Right. Forget I said anything."

She just nodded. "What is your name?"

Just in time I remembered not to give her my real name. "Sunset Val."

"What a cruel name to place upon a child." She snorted out grey smoke. The tiny exam room was starting to really stink. She picked up the bundle of cloth and tossed it at me. "I am Doctor Enerva. Put that on."

"Why?"

She let out a smoky sigh and glanced at the door. Or more specifically, at the goons we both knew were behind the door. I rolled my eyes and put on what turned out to be basically a stained baggy t-shirt that reached to my knees. When I unrolled it, an even filthier pair of slippers fell to the floor. I put those on, too. The shirt itched and the slippers were too big.

"What about my clothes?"

"Slaves own no property," she answered, crushing the cigarillo out under her booted foot. "Boys!"

The door opened and the goons looked in. They looked disappointed that they hadn't been called in to assist with my examination.

"Take her to be marked," the doctor ordered, packing her bag.

"Marked? What does that mean?" I asked as they dragged me off.

"You'll find out soon enough," one of the goons said.

Turned out being marked meant having a slave trader's mark tattooed on my left arm. I have nothing against tats. Never really wanted one myself, but if I'd had my choice it wouldn't have been a rough design of a crow in flight. And I wasn't exactly convinced their equipment met the cleanliness standards the tat parlours had back home. So, great! Infection, disease, gangrene, amputation, and a lifetime of being nicknamed Lefty.

It hurt like hell. They strapped me into a chair and by then my shock had worn off so I fought them, but they were big and huge and not exactly gentle. They drew the line at hitting me, though, so that was a small mercy. Still, the tattoo process wasn't pleasant at all.

The tattoo guy (I won't call him an artist, because he was more of a butcher) was small and old, with thick spectacles perched on his bulbous nose. "You're lucky you got took by Captain Crow," he told me in not-quite-Italian accented Anglic. "Other slavers, they still use branding. Not as fun as tattoo. Sometimes? The slaves, they pass out." He grinned at me, like it was a pretty good joke. Half his teeth were brown and rotting. I was too busy with the pain to grin back. Ha ha, people pass out from being branded like cattle, who knew?

Blood trickled down the length of my arm as the two goons led me away. They were built on the same design, big, muscular, and heavy. Scars criss-crossed their arms. The one on my right was bald and gap-toothed. The one on my left had maybe two weeks of black beard scrub on his face and lacked a finger on his left hand.

We went up a flight of stairs made of metal grating. Their booted feet clanged with every step. My slippered feet scuffed along between them. I was surprised how few people we encountered.

"Where is everyone?"

"Asleep," said the one on my right.

"Shut up, you." said the one on my left. He pinched the soft flesh behind my upper arm. The skin stretched, opening up the tattoo that had already begun to scab over. New blood trickled down my arm to join the drying blood already there. Plus, the pinch really hurt.

I know, I know, it could have been worse. He could have been slapping me around. I could have been raped and killed. It really could have been so much worse. But right there and then, I didn't care. I was miserable.

We came to an oval metal door with a central wheel for a doorknob. Rightside Goon turned the wheel while Leftside Goon held my poor, bleeding, pain-wracked arm. Like I was going to run away. Where would I run to, on a blimp high above the middle of an ocean on a planet I didn't belong on?

Rightside Goon opened the door. The first thing that hit me was the heat. A wave of it washed over me, making me realize how cold I actually was. The next thing that hit me was the smell, like a thousand locker rooms jammed into one. The smell of human bodies was so strong it actually made my eyes tear up.

"Don't fret none," Rightside Goon said. "You'll get used to yer new home right quick."

"Creedance, shut yer porthole," Leftside Goon said. He shoved me forward through the doorway. I almost tripped on the lip of the door, but caught myself before I fell.

"Nighty night," Leftside Goon laughed. Rightside, Creedance, closed the door.

It took a long time for my eyes to adjust to the darkness. The only light came from a single porthole off to my left. By the flashes of lightning, I could make out dozens of shapes in the dark, lying on low mats.

Women. Dozens of them.

Sharing a room with my sister, I'd come to realize that there are different kinds of sleep. There's normal sleep. There's the sleep when you're dreaming. And then there's the sleep of the truly exhausted. That's what these women were sleeping.

None of them woke up as I walked among them, trying to find a mat to lay down on. There were a few. Most of them were missing even the thin mattresses the other women were lying on. A couple of them had mattresses so filthy I didn't even bother. I was exhausted, but sleeping in someone else's sweat and pee and vomit and maybe even worse? No thanks.

Finally I found an empty mat that wasn't too horrible. I curled up on my side and fell right to sleep.

Chapter Eleven

Slavery Sucks. Period.

The next morning I woke up to the sound of a woman saying something angrily at me in a language I'd never heard before.

"Okay, okay, relax," I muttered as I sat up. Someone grabbed me by my wounded arm and hauled me to my feet. The scab opened up again and the pain woke me right up in a hurry.

"Hey!"

The dark-haired woman, dressed in a bright red blouse, a sleeveless knee-length coat buttoned up her stomach, tight slacks and thigh-high boots repeated herself, louder. Her volume wasn't in any kind of correlation to my comprehension. I shook my head.

"Anglic?" she asked.

"Um? Yeah!"

"Bah. Move!" To make sure I understood, she shoved me, hard enough to send me stumbling. My feet got tangled up in a mat, nearly tripping me.

The slave quarters were mostly empty. She shoved me into the line of women as they filed out of the room. None of them had woken me up. Really nice. Thanks a lot.

There were a couple of other goons in the corridor outside. The woman who'd woken me up came out last. They herded us along the corridors to a big room filled with tables and benches.

We lined up down one side of the room. No one spoke. Everyone kept their eyes down, trying to stay as inconspicuous as possible. I wound up dead last in line, so all I saw were women filing forward, toward something I couldn't see. Then the first ones in line hurried to the tables nearest the doors, carrying wooden bowls of something steaming and hunks of bread. From the spicy smell of the steam, I guessed it was some kind of stew.

The line moved forward quickly, and I soon discovered why they hadn't bothered to wake me up. As the last in line, I got the absolute last dregs scraped from the bottom of the cauldron, burned and nearly inedible.

The operative word being 'nearly'. I choked it down because I was absolutely starving. I hadn't eaten since a hurried supper the night before, a world away. A sharp pain filled my heart at the thought that I might never see home ever again, might never have my Mom's pasta sauce ever again, might never tell my sister to roll over because she was snoring ever again, might never complain that my idiot brother had left me stranded at my fencing class ever again.

Well, that last one wasn't true, at least. Even if I never got home again, I'd be complaining about being stranded by my stupid brother until the day I died, some old decrepit slave woman mouldering away in some Atlan manor home. They'd think I was crazy, talking about alternate worlds where there was no Atlan, no blimps except at football games, no Frankenstein nightmare girls, no...

"Eve!" I said out loud, standing up to look around, trying to spot her.

"No talking," one of the goons guarding us warned me.

I kind of ignored him. I couldn't see Eve anywhere, but she had to be around somewhere. They wouldn't have left her to rot somewhere, would they? Would she even rot, if they did?

"Hey!" the goon said. He walked toward me.

One of the women sitting next to me whispered something in that language I didn't understand. It kind of sounded Italian, or Spanish. Portuguese, maybe. Lucky me, I'd taken French as my language elective. I got the impression she was trying to help me, though.

The goon grabbed me by the back of my shirt and shoved me back to my seat.

"Ow!" I turned around to face him.

He shoved a thick finger in my face. "Shut it! No talking! No standing!"

I have to admit, what I did next wasn't very smart, but then, I was fed up of being ordered around. Surrounded by people who barely spoke English, or even Anglic. The only two people who knew where I was from, or how to get me back home, were gone. And this ugly sonuvabitch with his finger in my face?

I bit his finger.

I know, I know. Not smart. God knew where his finger had been, or what kind of germs I was putting in my mouth. Ugh, it made me sick just thinking about it.

Anyway, I bit him hard enough that his finger bled. He screamed like a girl, so unexpected from a huge goon like him that I let go and laughed.

That was the second thing I did that day that wasn't very smart. Being bitten by a slave was one thing, but being laughed at by a slave was something else entirely. He grabbed me with his good hand and hauled me to my feet, his hurt hand curling into a fist to lay into me. Hate and fury contorted his face into a Halloween mask of demonic intensity. I was dead.

A man's voice cracked across the silent crowd like the lash of a whip. "Karl!"

I watched sanity return to the goon's face, a bucket of ice water dumped on his raging fury. I looked to find my saviour.

He was one-eyed, tall, broad-shouldered, dressed in red and black. His unpatched eye was piercingly blue, his nose hooked, his dark hair cropped short. He moved with the easy stride of a man accustomed to being obeyed.

The goon growled. "Tyr, this bitch bit me!"

That one piercing eye just stared at the goon.

"Mr. Ebonfury," the goon said, eventually. "Sir. This slave assaulted me."

The eye stayed on the goon's face for a second longer than comfortable, then looked at me. He pitched his gravelly voice low, but the threat remained. "Is this true?"

My brain left my mouth running on autopilot. "I that is I mean he I was just looking for my friend Eve she was with me when you captured us I mean she's not really my friend but I kind of owe her my life sort of and and and he came along and shoved me down and stuck his finger in my face. So. I bit it?"

"Have the doctor look at the bite, Karl."

"Sir?"

The eye flicked back to Karl. He swallowed nervously, then dropped me to the floor and left.

"Get up," Tyr Ebonfury said to me. I stood up.

"Thanks, Mr. Ebonfury."

"Your name?"

"Val." Something about this guy made my brain fall out. "Sunset Val," I corrected myself, smiling, and offered my hand to shake. No sense getting off on the wrong foot with the guy who just probably saved me a beating, right?

He glanced at my hand, then stared at my face. Longer than comfortable. I dropped my hand, feeling my smile fade.

"Val is an odd patronymic," he said.

"So I'm told." Like he should talk?

"Sunset is an even odder name for parents to curse their daughter with."

"Well, they're pretty odd people."

"You're the girl we took last night."

"That's me. Have you seen the other girl with me? Is she okay?"

"The patchwork?" A smile flickered across his lips, then disappeared. "It's fine. It's in cold storage."

"Can I see her?"

"No."

"Please?"

A couple of the girls sitting near me snickered. I grinned.

Tyr Ebonfury didn't grin. "Assaulting a member of the crew is a week in the box. You're new. You might not have had the rules explained to you. As such, you'll only spend a day and a night in the box."

"What's the box?"

"After your stay, you'll stoke. One week."

"What's a stoke?" I asked, but he had already turned and left. A couple of the girls giggled, though at my words or at my predicament, I couldn't tell.

A huge hand clamped down hard on the back of my neck. "A day and a night in the box ought to shut that smart mouth of yours," an angry voice said. I glanced behind me. The goon looked enough like Karl that I guessed they were brothers.

The box was basically that. A small room, just long enough that I could either stretch out my legs or lie with my back flat on the metal floor, but not both, and not nearly tall enough for me to stand up straight. So narrow the side walls were almost touching my shoulders. No light penetrated the blackness, not even a thin slit around the door's edges. Worse, there was a rhythmic pounding that convinced me I must be near the ship's engines, just loud enough to be annoying.

At first I thought I could hack it. No big deal. I counted, I did math, I remembered states and their capitals, quoted from favourite movies, sang songs, got lost in my memories. I got thirsty, and tried to ignore it. Then I got hungry, and couldn't ignore both.

Then I started seeing things. Just glimpses of things at first. Flashes of light out of the corner of my eye. Flickers of movement in the dark. I closed my eyes but it changed nothing. The pounding, pounding, pounding noise, the flashes of light, the flickers of movement. The floor was hard and unforgiving.

I'll admit it, I cried. And drank my tears, I was so thirsty. There was nowhere for me to go to the bathroom, so I swore to myself I would hold it.

I suppose I must have fallen asleep at some point, because my own echoing nightmare screams woke me. I couldn't remember what the nightmares had been about, for which I was grateful.

By the time the door opened and light burned through my eyes and brain in painful stabbing brightness, I was so cramped up from being inside the box they had to drag me out and stand me up. They laughed at my cries of pain as blood began to circulate in my calves and feet.

My two guards, a man with a beard and a woman with the most awesome blonde curls, let me use a bathroom they called the privy. Basically it was a hole in a bench set in a cupboard, over another hole. Kind of a porta-potty, only permanent. A perma-potty. The stench was overpowering, but I held my breath and finished my business. There was nothing to wipe with but I was so relieved I didn't care.

The guards led me back to the mess hall. Most of the women there had already finished their meal, and looked up as I was marched in. I held my head up and back straight, determined not to show how close they'd come to breaking me.

I was also determined not to wind up in the box again.

I scraped the bottom of the cauldron with the big filthy copper ladle for all the burnt leavings I could find, then grabbed a seat and gobbled it down. It tasted disgusting but I was so hungry I didn't care. I had missed the end of the meal the day before, so I had no idea what happened when everyone was done eating. Basically it involved getting up and standing in line. Those closest the door got up and lined up first. As soon as they started lining up, the other women scrambled to finish their meals and line up too.

Of course, I had been the last one in, so I was the last one to line up. The second I joined the line, the blonde pirate with the curly hair started counting us off. The first five got cleaning detail. The next five got scouring.

The next five got swabbing. And so on, down the line. The last bunch of us got stoking. I still hadn't found out what stoking was.

The bearded pirate led us down a couple of flights of metal grating stairs. The pounding of the engines got louder and louder, until finally we couldn't even hear the sound of our feet on the metal floor. I was at the back of the line, so I moved up to walk next to one of the other women, a younger one, maybe twenty or so. It was hard to tell, she was so filthy. I suppose I must have been as well, but I hadn't seen a mirror since I'd arrived.

"What's stoking?" I whispered to her. She flinched away, then shook her head. Either she didn't understand me, or she didn't want to talk.

Anyway, I found out soon enough. We came to a huge room with four gigantic boilers. The room was as hot as an oven. Sweat trickled down my back in seconds. Overhead, enormous pistons drove a crankshaft the size of a street lamp. The pounding was hellishly loud. A pirate in stained overalls and clean circles around his eyes from the tinted goggles he had pushed up onto his forehead started yelling orders. His filthy face, filthy clothes and clean eyes made him look like an inverted raccoon. I almost giggled.

Some of the women who'd stoked before knew what to do. They took small shovels, barely bigger than both of my palms put together, and went to a large pile of what looked like black rocks. The pile rose at least twice my height, spilling from an open doorway. They shovelled the black rocks into dented metal pails about the size of the kind of bright plastic buckets a kid would use to make a sand castle. I grabbed a shovel and joined them, under the watchful eyes of the bearded pirate and Mr. Raccoon.

Mr. Raccoon waited until we all had a full pail, then went to one of the boilers, sliding his goggles into place. I thought it was hot in the room until he opened the boiler door. It went from hot as an oven to hot as hell. My eyes actually dried out when he opened the door. The glare from the boiler fires was a little like staring into the sun on a summer day. Retinal burns danced in front of me. I looked away as the other women shuffled forward into the killing heat and blinding light, tossed their bucket of black rocks into the boiler, and hurried back to the pile.

Lather, rinse, repeat. I'd like to say that a week of stoking passed in an exhausted blur. I'd like to say that, but I'd be lying. Every minute in the engine room passed like an hour, rendered deaf and mute by the pounding engines, blinded by the burning brilliance of the dancing fires, and then returning into the depths of darkness, seeking a black blurry shape in the shadows to shovel heavy lumps of what I eventually learned was not just coal but coke, a kind of concentrated coal, into the bucket and haul the heavy load to the fires once more, back-breaking and mind-numbing, a monotony that mesmerized and melted the mind of this mere mortal. Like I said, alliteration equals bad times for Val.

But somehow it didn't all blur. My first day stoking took hours of my young life away. Hours I would never get back, never see again. We were allowed to drink lukewarm, stale water from a barrel stored in the corner furthest from the engines, but only three times that day, and no lunch break. By the end I was parched, starving, my ears were ringing, I was filthy, and most of all, exhausted.

They marched us back up the stairs. One of the girls was too tired to make the climb, and stumbled. The other women ignored her, filing past. I stopped to help, grabbing her by the arm.

"Keep it moving, you!" the bearded pirate yelled.

"Hold on, she's hurt!"

She had a gash in her shin where she'd tripped into the metal grating of the step ahead, and the blood was trickling down her coke-blackened skin to soak her slipper. "I'm fine," she whispered to me. "Please. No fuss."

"Hurt is she?" Bearded said. "Can't have that. Diana!"

The pirate with the blonde curls stopped the women. She shoved her way through them along the narrow corridor to where we stood. "What?"

"This one's hurt," Bearded said. "Guess she goes to Dr. Enerva."

The blonde, Diana, raked a gloved hand through her blonde curls. She rolled her eyes in exasperation. "Blast it all, Pete."

Pete shrugged. "She tripped. I can't help it if she's a clumsy cow."

"The captain won't be happy about this."

"Think I don't know it?"

"I'll take her."

"Right then," Pete said, obviously relieved.

The girl I helped gave me a look that was equal parts hate and desperation as Diana dragged her back the way we'd come. Pete shoved me back into line.

"Where is she taking her?"

"Never you mind," Pete said. "Right you cows, get yer arses into the mess!"

The other women hurried forward. I stayed with Pete.

"What's going to happen to her? The girl, I mean?"

"She's gone to the doctor, hasn't she?"

"Will she be okay? Why is the captain going to be angry?"

He turned me around to march me into the mess. "Unharmed slaves fetch a higher price. If we get to market before she'd full healed, we lose money, get it?"

I turned to face him, walking backwards. "But what's wrong with Dr. Enerva?"

"Nothing's wrong with her," Pete said, but he looked around before answering, and his answer seemed forced, even though I was the only one who could have heard him. "Anyhow, get in the mess hall, you. You're last again."

Too tired to care, and more than a little worried about the girl I'd unwittingly sent to see Dr. Enerva, I got in line, got my burned scrapings of the same stew as the last two meals I'd had, and gobbled it down. I recognized chunks of carrot and potatoes, something that might have been onions. There were other things in the stew I didn't recognize, and I couldn't place the flavour of the couple of chunks of meat I found. I didn't think about it too much. Women were already lining up when I sat down to eat, so I had to hurry or be last in line again.

I wasn't last, but I might as well have been. Less than a handful of women were behind me in line. We filed through the corridors back to the slave quarters. The women who were first in line got the mats closest to the door. Since I was near the end, the mat I got was nowhere near the door. I'd have to get up extra early to beat the line up in the morning.

A single light bulb burned in the slave quarters, near the door and protected by a wire mesh cage. It was enough to see by, barely. There was a privy near me, and the smell nearly overpowered the stink of unwashed, sweaty bodies. Nearly, but not enough. Trapped between the two stenches, I wanted to vomit.

Instead, I lay down on my mat and tried to ignore the nausea. Women were talking, quietly, around me, a low murmur that I couldn't understand. None of them were speaking Anglic, so the sound of their voices became a white noise that lulled me to sleep.

My second day as a slave came to an exhausted end.

Chapter Twelve

Stoking the Fires

The rest of the week passed exactly the same as my second day aboard the pirate ship. My third day, I managed to get up early enough not to be last in line, so I managed to get an actual bowl of stew and not just the scrapings of the bottom. It tasted so much better, not burned. I finished up quick, then got in line again.

When it came time to assign tasks to us slaves, the blonde with the curls, Diana, gave me a look when she saw me almost at the front of the line.

"What do you think you're doing?" she asked.

"Getting in line?"

"Not you. You're on stoking the rest of the week, remember?" she said with a cruel smile, enjoying crushing my hopes. "I can have Karl remind you, if you need."

I rolled my eyes and went to the back of the line.

So, back to stoking I went. Most of the other women I'd stoked with on my second day managed to avoid being slow into line on my third day, so I was with a whole fresh batch. I helped them as much as I could, showing them the quick and dirty way of shovelling the coke into the buckets. You shoved the bucket right up against the pile of coke, holding it in place with your knees. Then you scraped the looser bits off the top of the pile, instead of trying to use the tiny, nearly useless shovels as actual shovels. You got coke on your lap and your legs got filthy, but it was less backbreaking that way.

I also helped them from going blind by showing them how to aim at the burning light and killing heat of the fire without staring directly at it, basically by keeping your eyes on the floor and using your peripheral vision.

I couldn't speak their language and the pounding of the engines would have made any attempts at speech pretty futile anyway, but a sort of makeshift sign language can go a long way. By the end of the third day, once we got back to the slave quarters, several of the women I'd helped came over and thanked me. I guessed it was thanking me, at least, because none of them spoke Anglic. I smiled and nodded a lot. I looked around but there was no sign of the girl with the gashed shin. I hoped she was okay as I crawled onto my mat, which was a little closer to the door. Sleep came in seconds. Morning came in seconds too, or at least, that's how it seemed.

That's pretty much how the next few days went by. Knowing I was going to be stoking, I took my time with my meals, though I was quick to line up to get to the mess and back to our quarters again, getting closer to the door each night. I was determined to seem like the perfect little slave, because I had plans.

Escape plans.

I wasn't sure how, or when, but I knew I'd get out of there. Somehow. I wasn't going to spend the rest of my life as a slave on some world that wasn't my own. I was going to get home.

Somehow.

First step, make the pirates underestimate me. I did this by following orders quickly and without complaint. Second step, get the other slaves to like me, despite the language barrier. I did this by being helpful and smiling a lot. My face ached sometimes, from smiling at the other women, making faces when the pirates' backs were turned, that sort of thing. I ingratiated myself with them.

Or at least, most of them. Some of the women wouldn't meet my eye. And some of the women were just bitches who didn't like me. But most of them were terrified of winding up as slaves in some Atlan pleasure house.

My first week was almost up when something new and interesting happened. I had almost settled into a routine, too, but anything new and interesting was a welcome change. What happened was, about halfway through the day, an alarm sounded. At least, I'm going to assume it sounded, we couldn't hear anything in the engine room. But a light began to flash overhead, and the pirate engineer, the one I'd thought of as Mr. Raccoon and whose name was actually Luke, looked startled. Then he ordered us to stop shovelling and go stand in one corner. He wiped his filthy face with a filthier rag, not really cleaning anything, and we waited while Luke checked the gauges on the boilers. He licked his lips nervously.

Suddenly the engine room door opened and maybe two dozen more slaves entered the room, guarded by just two pirates. Karl was one. I recognized the other, a big black dude with dreadlocks, but didn't know his name.

As soon as the slaves were all crowding around us, Karl and Dreads closed the door. I saw the wheel turn. They'd locked us in.

Three dozen slaves, and only Luke to watch over us.

It seemed pretty obvious to me that we outnumbered him like crazy. I got the impression he knew it, too, because for the first time all week he picked up one of those little shovels. It seemed a pretty ineffective weapon against all of us.

It wouldn't even take all of us. Four or five of us could take him down, easy. If I had my epee I could have taken him out by myself. I just needed to find the right women for the job.

Luke looked over at a huge dial set on the wall. Over it was a bank of light bulbs, each bigger than my fist. The lights suddenly flared to life, and the dial spun. It stopped with a red triangle at the top. Inside the triangle were written the letters MXA.

Luke started yelling at us. His voice was surprisingly high for a guy as big as him, and I snickered. I know, it wasn't very nice, but then, he hadn't been especially nice, either.

He threw open all of the boiler doors and yelled at us to feed as much coke as possible into the fires. At first we all ran this way and that, a nightmare of women scrambling in every direction, trying to get out of each other's way and just running into other women doing the same. Luke just kept yelling at us, his high voice piercing the incessant pounding of the engine.

I pulled myself out of the mob and started organizing the scrambling women, making the ones carrying coke pass on my left while the ones coming from the boilers returned to the pile via my right. At first it was like herding cats. None of the women wanted to listen to me. They were terrified of Luke and his high voice and that little shovel. I'd spent a week under his less than watchful eye, knowing he was a lazy ass and probably a coward to boot, given how often he glanced at the dial, the door, and us women. Dial, door, dial, door, dial, door, women. He was barely paying attention to us.

If I could just speak their stupid language we totally could have jumped him, then waited for whoever came to relieve him to open the door, and then we'd be able to take the ship! But how do you lead a bunch of people who not only don't understand you, but don't want to be led?

Eventually I got a proper line of women stoking into the first boiler, bringing coke faster than the mad scramble going on at the other boilers. I grabbed a woman who I recognized from stoking earlier in the week and put her in charge of making sure the line stayed organized, then moved on to the next boiler.

The whole floor shook and several women lost their footing. I helped up a couple as I moved to the next boiler. With the first boiler line serving as an example, it was much easier to get the second line organized. The third boiler was even easier. But when I got to the fourth boiler, Luke finally noticed what I was doing and decided to take offence.

At least, that's what I figured his yelling and waving that little shovel in my face was all about. How dare I stop stoking to organize? How dare I pull other women off the stoking to keep the organization from falling apart? Get to work, you lazy cow! That sort of thing. Not that I understood a word of it. The big jerk actually shoved me into the pile of coke. I lacerated the palm of my hand in the process. I looked at the blood, so bright red against my filthy black hands, then looked up at Luke.

He looked like he was going to be sick. He'd made a slave bleed.

Worse, he'd seriously pissed me off.

I jumped up and ran at him, shoving him hard. He stumbled back, more from surprise than from the force of my tackle. He wound up backing into the boiler. I'm sure it was my imagination, but I could have sworn I heard the sizzle of his bare back frying against the hot metal. He screamed just like Karl.

Then he swung that little shovel at my head. I ducked under it and glanced around for something to fight him back. One of the girls tossed me a little shovel of my own. I parried his next lunge and riposted with one of my own. As a fencer, he sucked. He just swung wide and hard, telegraphing every attack and following through like a bull charging a rodeo clown. Which I suppose made me the clown.

I tapped him a few times in the ribs and gut, easily avoiding his attacks and really just playing with him. He caught me with a lucky shot against my shoulder, hard enough that I almost dropped the shovel in the pain that followed. That's when it really sunk in. He could kill me. I could die. At best, if he won he'd just beat me bloody, maybe break some bones. I didn't want to be beaten. I didn't want to be bloody. I didn't want to have bones broken. And I most especially didn't want to die.

I stopped playing with him. He caught the flat of my shovel blade square in the face, smashing his nose into a splay of blood. The whole room shifted again, and we stumbled into each other. He tried to trap me in a bear hug and I jumped hard on his foot. I ran up the pile of coke and grabbed a pipe hanging overhead, one I knew from experience had cold water running through it and not scalding steam. I swung over him to land on the stairs to the door.

And that's when I saw the women cheering me on.

Luke stalked up the stairs, a shovel in each hand, blood streaming down his face to stain his already filthy overalls. I backed away, shifting my grip on the shovel.

To my left, the bank of lights flashed blindingly bright and the dial spun, only to land back on MXA. Luke's filthy face paled and he forgot all about me, running back down the stairs to yell at the women. They went back to their lines, scrambling to avoid him and the flat of his shovels, which he suddenly wasn't afraid to use on the women's backsides. I yelled at them to fight him, fight back, do SOMETHING, but they couldn't hear, or wouldn't listen.

I stayed where I was with my back to the door. Luke stayed near the boilers, glaring at me. Without anyone to organize them, gradually the neat orderly lines of women stoking devolved into the random mess it had been when we started.

When the lights flashed and the dial spun again, it stopped on RGM. Luke stopped the women stoking and closed the boiler doors, then forced them all to stand over in a corner. I stayed on the stairs.

Not long after, the door opened behind me. Diana and Dreads stepped through. I whirled on them, shovel en garde. Dreads did something with his hands too quick for me to see, but suddenly I didn't have the shovel any more. Diana grabbed me and shoved me face first into the wall, my arm twisted behind my back. I had enough presence of mind to keep my wounded palm closed. I didn't want to be sent to Dr. Enerva, like the girl who'd disappeared.

"OW!"

Dreads yelled something at Luke, who yelled something back. From his tone, I could guess what Dreads was saying. You let this little girl beat you up?! And Luke was all, Yeah, you try keeping these stupid cows in line, see how you like it!

Diana leaned in close, close enough that I felt her breath on my ear. "It's the box again for you. Don't worry, though. This time you'll have company."

"Company?! There was barely enough room for me in that hole!"

Dreads got the women lined up and filing out of the engine room.

"Not in the same box, stupid," Diana said. "We have more than one box. No, we pretty much had to put your new neighbour into the box right away."

"Why?"

"Let's just say she'd spoil in the sunlight."

"What does that mean?"

Diana leaned over to look at my face, puzzlement clear on her features. "Are you being deliberately dense?"

"No, look, seriously, I have no clue what you mean."

Diana frowned. "What kind of person spoils in the sunlight?"

"Emo goths?"

She paused. "What language was that?"

"Never mind. I don't know who spoils in sunlight."

"Vampyri?" she said like it was totally obvious. She pronounced it 'vom-pee-ree'.

I played along. "OH! Right. I … um, never met one."

Diana gave me a good long look, a look that said, you're such a weirdo, and what kind of weirdo are you, and you're quite possibly more trouble than you're worth, even if you are a redhead and will fetch a good price at market, what with not speaking Atlan, attacking two crewmen, and all the odd questions.

Possibly I'm extrapolating a little.

Once all the other women had been marched out of the engine room, Diana hauled me off the wall. One hand on my shoulder and another on the arm she kept twisted behind me, Diana forced me out of the engine room. But before I left, I couldn't help myself. I grabbed the door jamb and shot a look over my shoulder, knowing Luke would be watching us. I gave him the most triumphant grin I had, and even shot him a peace sign with my fingers. The fact that it also looked like a V (for Val, see?) was definitely a pleasure, but not as great as seeing the confusion on his face. Why would a slave be so happy to be going to the box?

Diana shoved me hard and I went. I hated the idea of being in the box again but loved the memory of all the women cheering me on as I kicked Luke's ass.

Chapter Thirteen

New Friend, Old Enemy

The box was as bad as I remembered, but only for a couple of hours.

Why a couple of hours, you ask? Well, for one, after a couple of hours my neighbour woke up. I know this because there was a sudden noise, which I thought I recognized as someone trying to sit up in the box and banging their head, pretty much on account of the fact that I'd done it myself, my first time in. Whoever she was, she swore in yet another language I didn't recognize. Ever notice how you can always tell when someone is swearing, even in a different language? Anyhow, she swore, and then there was a bunch of noises as she tested the limits of her prison. Then more swearing and even some pounding on the walls. She was really strong, judging by the volume of her pounding. When I banged on the metal walls, I could barely make a noise.

I waited for a lull in the swearing and pounding, and yelled over the sound of the engine below us. "Hello? Can you hear me? Do you speak English? I mean, Anglic?"

Her words came quick and accented. "Who are you? Vhy am I here? Vhere am I?"

"Listen, my name is Val, Sunset Val. We're both prisoners of a gang of pirates who are also slavers. Lucky us, am I right?"

"Vhich pirates?"

"Huh?"

"Vhich. Pirates."

"Oh. Sorry. Not used to your accent. Um, I don't know the name of the pirates. Well, that is, I know some of them. I've only been here a week."

"The captain. Who is the captain?!"

"He says his name is Captain Crow."

Another string of swears came from her.

"Listen, um, what's your name?"

"I am Serena Heartlace."

And everyone thinks I have a weird name? "Okay, so, Serena, you know this Captain Crow?"

"Of him, yes."

"And he's bad news?"

"He is vun of the most successful slavers in the vorld. How amazing that he should be the vun to take us, since ve have been looking for him."

"Looking for him vhy? I mean, why?"

"I vas vorking vith a group of emancipationists."

"Who?"

"People who believe slavery to be wrong."

"Well, yeah, no duh. Slavery sucks."

"I am gratified to hear you say this. It is a wery rare thing."

"Yeah, I get that. So, what do you figure is going to happen to us?"

"I have no idea. I vas slumbering vhen I vas taken."

"You must be a pretty heavy sleeper," I said.

I heard her laugh. It was high and pretty. "Yes. Wery heavy. As are all my kind."

Her kind? "Oh right, one of the pirates said you were vompeeree."

"Wampyri," she corrected me. Hearing it in her accent, it finally clicked.

Mad scientists. Frankenstein girls. Why not a vampire?

"So uh... you're a vampire?"

"Wampyri, yes."

"You drink blood?"

"As do all my kind, of course."

"With claws and fangs and all that?"

"Fangs, yes. I do not understand vhere you humans, and I assume you are human? I do not understand vhere this ridiculous legend comes from. No wampyri has ever had claws. Honestly, ve are not beasts."

"But you drink human blood."

"Do you eat meat?"

"Well, yeah."

"Does that mean you have claws?"

"Look, I get it. So what about mirrors, holy symbols, death by sunlight, all that?"

"Have you never met vun of my kind?"

"I can honestly say never."

"Mirrors vork fine. Holy symbols are not anathema to us. The sun, however, is to be avoided. Direct sunlight can burn us terribly, even kill. Indirect sunlight vill not kill us, so long as ve can vithstand the slumber, the curse that puts us to sleep when the sun rises. That is the truth behind the legend of our daytime wulnerability."

"Do stakes in the heart kill you? Or beheading?"

"Vouldn't they kill you as vell?"

"Okay, yeah, good point."

She found that hilarious. Eventually I got the joke. Stakes, good point, ha ha? I was tired enough that I laughed too.

We were quiet for a while, then I asked, "So if you're vampyri, why didn't they just chuck you overboard? Aren't you going to be serious trouble for them once we get to market?"

"Bah. They vill vait until daylight and the slumber takes me. Then they vill take me out of this box and put me in another. Besides, I doubt they vill feed me. I vill veaken vithout feeding. Even if they are so foolish as to release me from this forsaken box during the night, I vill be in no condition to fight them. And they have taken all my veapons."

"Veapons? I mean, weapons? You fight?"

"Of course. I am a swordmistress of the ninth order. I am studying to be accepted into the eighth order next Septimus. I do not fear that I vill be rejected."

"You're like the first woman I've met who fights. Except for the women pirates, I guess. All the others on board, the slaves? They won't fight back. We outnumber them like five to one. We could take them easy."

"I do not doubt that most of the vomen taken as slaves came from genteel families vhere the varrior training vas left to the menfolk and the care and maintenance of the household left to the vomen. It is a foolish conceit."

"No kidding." I thought for a moment. The other women had cheered me, when I fought Luke. If I could hold off Luke as long as I did with just a shovel, what could I do with an actual sword? How many of them would I have to take out before the others rose up against our pirate captors?

"Listen, Serena."

"I am listening, Sunset Wal."

"If I can get you out, will you help me?"

"Help vith vhat?"

"Overtake this ship, free the other slaves, all that?"

"If you can get me out of this box, I vill do more than that. But I vill be veak. I vill need blood."

Nervously, I licked my parched lips with a tongue that was drying out, trying not to think of the scab forming on my palm. "You let me worry about that."

"Wery vell. I swear to you by my blade, free me and ve vill take command of this ship and free the slaves. Free me, and I am yours to direct as you vill."

"Awesome."

"Have you a plan?"

"I will by the time they let me out."

We talked a little while, but unfortunately for my planning, the day had exhausted me and I fell asleep not long after. When I woke up, Serena slumbered, which she'd explained was kind of like a temporary coma, a defence mechanism that protected her entire species from risking being exposed to the lethal sun. Pretty much nothing would wake her up once she was taken by the slumber.

While she was slumbering, the door to my box opened. The light was so bright it was like being slapped in the face. I raised my hand to shield my eyes and shrank back from the light. A rough hand grabbed my ankle and dragged me out of the box.

"None of that, you," Karl said. "Captain wants to talk."

"Great, I need to make a complaint about the accommodations," I answered as he hauled me to my feet.

"Keep yer mouth shut."

"Or you'll what? Slap me around? We both know you can't risk damaging the merchandise."

He leaned in close, close enough for me to smell the stink of his breath. "I can make your life hell, little girl."

I wasn't going to back down to this goon, though. "What can you do that hasn't already been done to me? The box? Stoking?"

"You little..."

"Yeah, yeah, whatever. Let's keep the Captain waiting while you think up a suitable retort, sound good?"

I could actually hear his teeth grinding over the sound of the engines below us. I grinned my cheekiest grin at him.

He grabbed my shoulder and turned me around, then marched me along corridors and up stairwells. I got a little lost in all the twists and turns, but

I counted at least a half dozen stairwells, which put us at least three levels over the slave quarters. The air got cooler and less foul.

This level was a lot nicer than any of the others I'd seen up until then. Elegant electric lamps lined the hall on both sides. The floor had a thin worn carpet running the length. There were even a couple of paintings hanging on the walls. As we passed them, I glanced at them. Nothing I recognized.

We came to a large set of double doors, made of actual wood. The brass door handles were shaped like two crows facing each other. Karl reached past me and turned one, yanking the door toward us.

Frigidly cold air greeted us, raising gooseflesh on my bare arms and legs. I didn't care. I felt a breeze for the first time in days, and man, had I ever missed it. I closed my eyes and breathed in sweet fresh air.

Then Karl gave me a shove. I stumbled forward and nearly tripped up a flight of wooden stairs.

"Hey! Watch the merchandise!"

"Get going, you," he rumbled through clenched teeth.

I turned to look at him and found no reassurance at all in what I saw. Pure murderous hate seeped out of his every pore, shining bright and mad in his piggy eyes.

I glanced over his shoulder, hoping someone would come by. "Um, where are you taking me?"

"Captain wants to see you," he said. Yeah, right.

"Where is he?"

"On deck." Again: yeah, right.

I started backing away from him, up the stairs. Once out of the stairwell, my first thought was that we must be sailing through a fog, but then I realized, hello, we're flying? The thick clammy wetness all around us, hiding the ship from view, must be a cloud.

And I couldn't hear any sounds of any other crew. "Where is everybody?"

"Mess hall," Karl answered, stalking towards me.

"The captain doesn't want to see me, does he?"

Karl's reply was a cruel smile that held no humour. At least, none to share. Then the smile disappeared, and the look on his face was even scarier than what I'd seen in the stairwell. "You made a fool of me."

"Oh, you didn't need any of my help."

"You rotten little cow!" he snarled, then rushed me, arms high.

Pure instinct took over and I sidestepped his charge. It wasn't as elegant as a matador avoiding an enraged bull, but the effect was similar. Plus I guess I misjudged how fast he was going, because he clipped my foot with his own. As a result, he tripped and skidded along the metal deck. I nearly went down too, but managed to keep my footing. Barely.

He scrambled to his feet. Like a dummy, I stood there watching instead of running. A small part of my brain couldn't believe this was happening. This guy wanted to kill me because I bit his finger. It sounds ridiculous to say it out loud like that, but that was exactly what was happening.

When he whirled around, spotted me, and charged again, the rest of my brain told the rational, logical part, the part that couldn't believe what was happening, to shut the hell up, and took over. Short version? I ran for it.

Of course, I had no clue where I was going, and couldn't see much past ten or twelve feet in front of me. He knew the ship as well as any deck hand. Also, the cloud did funny things to sound, so the sounds of his boots against the deck were muffled. I could have turned around to try and see how close or far he was, but I figured it was a better idea to keep an eye on where I went.

I climbed coils of rope, ducked under pipes and rigging and what looked like a giant unloaded harpoon gun. I came to a wall with a metal ladder, briefly considered climbing it, then turned to my right and narrowly ducked my attacker's swatting arms. I yelped and nearly fell, but caught myself and scrambled away, back the way I'd come.

If I could find the stairwell again I might be able to lose him in the corridors below deck. Of course, I couldn't exactly see anything, and had been a little busy avoiding being killed to keep track of where I had been going. It wasn't very long at all before I realized I must have missed the stairwell.

Karl appeared suddenly out of the cloud, a huge, cruelly barbed hook in his bandaged hand.

"I'm going to gut you like a fish," he promised.

Cornered as I was between a capstan and a rigging rack, I really didn't have very many options. The last time I'd tried to climb away from a problem I'd been drugged and chained up. I got the impression that Karl was in no mood to be that polite.

Luckily for me, Karl was kind of gigantic and I was kind of smallish, so I figured I would go for broke and try something that only works in the movies. I dived for his legs, hoping to slide right through them.

Yeah, it only works in the movies. I crashed right into his legs. Caught off guard at my unexpected attack, he tripped over me, stumbled and fell.

Right onto the hook.

Chapter Fourteen

Another Thing the Movies Don't Tell You

In the movies, someone who stumbles onto a huge hook just sort of lies there. The hero goes to them and turns them over to reveal the hook sticking out of his chest. Maybe there's a splash of something that kind of looks like blood on his shirt. Depending on the genre, there are a couple of options as to what happens next. In a horror movie, the hooked guy sits up and attacks the hero. In a comedy, the hooked guy maybe gets off a couple of coughs and a snappy one-liner. In an action movie, the hooked guy has just enough strength to cough up some fake blood, realize the error of his ways and tell the hero the tidbit of information the hero has been looking for. Maybe it's where they're keeping the hero's love interest. Maybe it's the villain's secret weakness, or the way into the hidden fortress.

None of that happened. Karl moaned for a bit, struggled to get up, gurgled and fell back to the deck, which was rapidly becoming a bloody mess, as my tormentor leaked his life out.

I stood there and watched him die.

I'd like to say I tried to help him, but I can't, because I didn't. I think I was in shock. I didn't go to him, didn't turn him over, didn't do CPR like I had learned in Phys. Ed., keeping him alive until Dr. Enerva came and took over, telling me I'd saved his life. He didn't learn from the error of his ways, becoming my new protector.

He died.

And all I could think was, *Good*.

A hand clamped down on my shoulder, scaring the hell out of me. Maybe I yelled a little, I don't remember.

Creedance spun me around to face him. His gap-toothed smile was gone. He ran his free hand over his bald head, features unreadable as he looked at Karl's corpse and the rapidly cooling pool of blood. "You'll have to answer to the Captain for that."

"It was an accident!"

"Save it for the Captain."

He shoved me ahead of him, past the corpse. Down the stairwell, which it turned out was only feet from where Karl had trapped me. Along the corridors. We came to another set of double wooden doors, again with the brass crow handles.

A man yelled, "Come!"

I felt numb, completely numb. All thoughts of escape had evaporated. A man was dead because of me. And part of me, hell, most of me, was okay with that. What kind of person was I?

Creedance opened the door and shoved me through. I stumbled and fell to my knees. People laughed. I looked up.

Captain Crow sat at the head of a long wooden table that was heavily laden with every delicious food imaginable, from roasts to pastries, cakes and pies. Bottles lined a sideboard. It looked like what the slop they served the slaves lacked in originality was more than compensated for on the crew's menu. Several crew members were there: Dreads and Diana, Tyr Ebonfury and Dr. Enerva, the nasty bearded guy who'd been with Creedance the night I was captured, that other dark-haired woman pirate. From the way Tyr was holding and kissing Dr. Enerva's hand, it was pretty obvious they were together.

"Karl's dead," Creedance said. The laughter stopped.

Captain Crow leaned forward. "Is he now?"

"Yessir."

"How? I must assume this little one is in some way connected to our companion's untimely demise."

"Yessir."

I got to my feet. Creedance shoved me back down to my knees. "He was going to kill me!"

"Was he now? And pray tell, why?"

"Because of that time I bit his finger? And he screamed like a girl in front of all the slaves. He said I made a fool of him. I told him he didn't need my help."

Dreads laughed once, a short bark of grim humour. Tyr smirked. I got the impression Karl wasn't much liked.

Captain Crow leaned back in his throne-like chair, his bony fingers steepled in front of his face. "Under normal circumstances, the price for killing a member of the crew is a long, slow, painful death at the hands of our dear doctor."

I glanced at Dr. Enerva. She looked especially excited at the idea, looking at me like I was a new rat for her lab.

"However..." The Captain leaned forward again, placing his chin on his palm and tapping his long nose with one bony finger. Dr. Enerva suppressed a sigh and turned back to canoodling with Tyr.

"You're in luck today, my dear," Captain Crow said. "Quite aside from the fact that you weren't the first piece of merchandise that our dearly departed Karl was suspected of doing away with, your particular shade of hair colour makes you something of a rarity where we're going. As such you'll fetch a handsome price. You've made a nuisance of yourself to Master Luke, so no more stoking for you. No, you'll sort our stock for the next three days."

"What happens in three days?"

The Captain looked at his crew like they were all in on some private joke. "We arrive at market, of course."

Chapter Fifteen

Inhuman Allies

Sorting turned out to be not that bad.

Backbreaking and supervised by the tattoo artist, the tiny old bespectacled guy who insisted we call him Mister Shorty. And he was, too, even shorter than me. On top of that, Mister Shorty was a micro-managing pain in the butt.

"Lift with your knees, you cow! Where did you put that keg of rum? Not there, here! You, Fatty, get your arse over here and help with this crate. Everyone push on the same side. Count those cans of stewed prunes again. Not with your left hand!"

Mister Shorty was the only one allowed to hold the crowbar we used to open the wooden crates and travelling cases the pirates had stolen from the ships they'd taken. There was everything you could imagine in the crates and cases, from machine parts to fine clothing. Mister Shorty would open one up, two of us would lift the top off, and we'd all dig in, pulling everything out while another girl made notes while Mister Shorty made sure we didn't cheat the inventory.

And man, what an inventory. The Booty Hold (I swear that's what they called it, I wouldn't make that name up) was easily the second biggest room I'd seen on the ship. Bigger than the Engine Room, even, and crammed to the rafters with stuff. The only room bigger was the launch bay for the ornithopters, which pretty much made up the rest of the same deck the Booty Hold was on.

I quickly came to understand why I'd been put on sorting as a punishment. Mister Shorty ran us ragged, and we weren't brought back to the mess for our meals. Dreads brought a small cauldron of that slop they fed us and we all ate from it, quick as we could without making ourselves sick. We passed around a bucket of warm water to wash it down. Then it was right back to work.

They didn't even bother marching us back to the slave quarters to sleep. Mister Shorty just kept us working past lights out, until we were staggering from fatigue. Then he told us to get some rest. Most of the girls lay down on the pile of rugs and carpets we had rolled and stacked. I just collapsed where I stood and was out like a light.

Mister Shorty got us up before dawn, and it was another day of sorting and stacking, opening crates and cases and counting inventory. It would have been like Christmas or a birthday party, if any of it had been for us. As it was, it was just work. Which was too bad, since there were some things I would have loved.

My second day sorting they added more girls to our work force, bringing our numbers to nearly two dozen. I was so busy unpacking a crate of machine parts that I didn't notice the new girl next to me until she handed me a gear the size of a dinner plate. When our hands brushed each other, I thought, *Fuzzy?*

I glanced at her hand. It was fuzzy. Or, more precisely, covered in a fine ginger fur. Her palm had those rough pads you'd see on the bottom of cat's feet. My eyes followed her furry arm all the way up to a cat's face, if cats were the size of humans.

Then she spoke. "You know, it's rude to stare."

I'm pretty sure I just blinked at her, my mouth gaping open like a fish. A catgirl. An honest to God catgirl. One that spoke Anglic, too, even if it was a little accented with a not-quite-French accent.

That's when I started to doubt my sanity, just a little. Maybe I hadn't been transported to another world by a mad scientist and his patchwork daughter. Maybe I hadn't been captured and enslaved by airship pirates. Maybe I hadn't had a conversation with a vampire and hadn't killed a man who was going to kill me. Maybe, just maybe, I was lying in a hospital somewhere, completely stark raving delusional, drugged to the gills, my parents weeping at the fate of their poor crazy daughter, who they'd never fully understood.

"At least, that's what people keep telling me," the catgirl said. She grinned impishly, an odd human mannerism on her feline features. Her fangs looked extremely sharp. "I just can't help it, you know? I like to know stuff. That's why I studied engineering. Not that it will do me much good where we're going, I suppose. Still, better to know stuff and not need it, than need to know stuff and not know it."

"You're a cat!" Yep, that's me, mistress of the obvious.

"I beg your pardon, I'm an animan. That my makers saw fit to bless me with cat attributes is something for which I'm forever grateful, but I am not a cat girl."

"Ani-man? But, I mean, you are a girl, right?"

You know that look cats get when they're watching you and you've done something stupid? She gave me that look. "You're a girl, and you're a *hu*-man."

"Okay, whatever, I just never heard of animans before."

Her green eyes went wide in her ginger face. "You've never heard of animen?"

"Uh, I mean, we don't see them a lot where I come from."

"But you have heard of us?"

In anime and comic books, sure. "Oh, yeah. I've just never seen one up close before."

She preened, turning her head so that I could get a good look. "I'm Meliora Fantastico Lyon, but people call me Gigi."

"Hi." I handed her the gear she'd handed me as Mister Shorty walked past us with a critical eye. I waited until he busied himself criticizing some of the newer girls on their stacking skills. "I'm Sunset Val."

"What an intriguing name!"

"Um, thanks."

"Ooo look!" she said, and leapt to the next crate.

Most of the crates we'd been opening were on the smallish, squarish side. Easily carried by one big guy or two slave girls. Three or four in the case of the crates of machine parts. The box that Gigi jumped over to was easily six feet long by three feet high by four feet wide. It had writing in Atlan all over it, which Gigi obviously read, though she must have been near-sighted to need to press her nose? snout? Do cats have snouts? Anyhow, to put her face so close to the writing.

Gigi gasped. "Quick quick quick! Help me open this one!"

I went over and grabbed one edge. Gigi fingertips grew claws and she sunk them under the edge on the other side of the crate. Mister Shorty had gone around crowbarring the crates all morning, so we just had to unlid them, take out the stuff inside, and inventory it.

Gigi and I lifted the lid up and slid it along the crate. The lid alone weighed a ton. I couldn't imagine how they got it aboard ship.

The crate was filled with the wood shavings that I'd learned served the same role as those foam packing chips did back home. Gigi jumped into the crate and dug around the packing shavings until she felt something, then she heaved.

"Help me!" she said excitedly.

I reached into the packing shavings and felt for whatever it was she was so excited about. I felt something cold and metallic. I grabbed onto an edge and heaved with Gigi.

It was a robot. Shaped like a girl. Actually, shaped like a maid.

I felt I had to ask the obvious question, not sure I wanted to know the answer. "Why's it shaped like a maid?"

Gigi didn't take her eyes off the robot, inspecting every inch. She had a pretty face, for a robot. "What else would an automaidon be shaped like?"

"A what?"

"Automaidon? Automaton maid of all work? No?" That did get her attention away from her examination. "Where are you from? The moon?"

"Might as well be," I muttered, but Gigi didn't hear me.

"Of course, if you were from the moon, you'd be one of those giant bugs they have up there," she went on smoothly.

"You're joking, right? Tell me there isn't giant bugs on the moon."

Gigi burst into a fit of kitty giggles, covering her mouth with her hands. "Sorry, I couldn't help it."

I laughed too.

She turned back to the automaidon. "Argenta."

"What?"

"The instructions said her name is Argenta."

"It has a name?"

"Of course." She grabbed one of the robot's arms. "Come on, we have to keep her from these, these, these villains."

"Are you kidding again? We could barely pull her into a sitting position. You want to get her out of the box?"

"Help me!"

What else could they do to me? In two days I was going to be sold to some sicko with a thing for redheads. I grabbed Argenta's arms while Gigi climbed around behind her to push.

We got the inactivated robot into a standing position. Her wide metal skirt wasn't especially conducive to keeping her balanced.

"Why are we doing this?"

Gigi glanced around to make sure Mister Shorty was still busy with the other girls. "Automaidons aren't worth very much on the black market. Too easy to track, you see?" She started leaning Argenta over the edge of the crate. "But you can take them apart and sell them for their individual parts. Lots of people are looking for spare bits and pieces. It would be a crime to take Argenta apart. She's a real work of art."

I grabbed Argenta and kept her from falling over. She wasn't too heavy, just really awkward. And how she would keep her balance once activated was beyond me. "But where are we going to hide her?"

"I can get her up and running in a couple of hours, with the right tools."

"We don't! Watch it! Have a couple of hours, Gigi."

"I know! Here. No here." She grabbed my hand and put it on Argenta's waist. "You'll have to cover for me."

"Cover for you? Gigi, listen to me. We need a plan." I thought for a second. "If I cover for you, will you help me revolt?

"Revolt?" she whispered. "We'll all be killed. Or worse."

"Not if I can get some friends to help."

"What friends?"

I told her about Eve and Serena. "If we can get them out of where they're being held, we can totally revolt."

But Gigi didn't need convincing. "We can use Argenta to get your patchwork out of cold storage, then sneak away to the box and get the vampyri out. But one needs electricity and the other needs blood. How are we going to feed them both?"

"You figure something out for Eve. I'll take care of Serena."

Chapter Sixteen

Weapons Come in All Shapes and Sizes

Covering for Gigi was easier than I thought. I just had to work twice as hard.

She came out of hiding for the evening meal, then disappeared again. I unpacked crates and piled stuff and sorted things and counted all kinds of crap. Some stuff looked interesting. Some stuff looked boring. I didn't care either way. All I knew was the revolt was coming. Even if we failed, at least I'd go down swinging.

Sometime past midnight, I collapsed on a pile of coats.

"Last night in the Booty Hold, girls," Mister Shorty announced as I drifted off to sleep. "Tomorrow you're for the grooming and a good meal and a good night's sleep."

That woke me up. We didn't have two days to get the revolt going, we had tonight! I waited until Mister Shorty's turned his back then slid off the pile of coats and sneaked off.

Finding Gigi turned out to be a lot harder than I might have expected. First of all, I had to keep extra quiet, and avoid Mister Shorty, who kept on working even after all the girls were gently snoring the sleep of the truly exhausted. For an old dude, he sure had a lot of energy. He kept getting up from his bench and shambling along the piles of stuff, picking out the choicest pieces and carrying them back to his bench, amassing quite a pile in the process.

But I didn't have time to take an inventory. Avoiding Mister Shorty took a lot of effort and attention, and half my attention was taken up, trying to find a cat that didn't want to be found.

Luckily my ears were better than Mister Shorty's. I heard the clatter of metal on metal, soft and muted but just loud enough to hear, not far away, and headed for it. I also heard a little muttered rowling, like, well, like an angry cat.

I finally found Gigi under a stack of crates that had been piled up around Argenta's crate, which had been turned on its side, open end facing the wall.

It made a kind of hidden cave, with just enough room to crawl in and out again. I poked my head through the opening to see a real mess. Wires were criss-crossed everywhere. Most of them were hooked up to something that kind of looked like a car battery the size of a television set. The other end of many of the wires snaked into Argenta's back.

A hiss and a snarl and a swipe of claws I narrowly dodged, banging my head in the process, alerted me to Gigi's presence.

"Oh! It's you," she whispered, as if she hadn't just tried to claw my eyes out. "I've almost got her ready for a trial run."

"No time for a trial run. It's Go Time, right now."

"I'm sorry?"

"We've got to get this revolution going. Tomorrow we're going to be groomed, whatever that means. All I know is, we're out of the Booty Hold in the morning."

Once again, I noticed the barriers of language couldn't stop the inflection of swearing. Gigi let loose a string of words, then covered her mouth and apologized wordlessly. I shrugged and smiled. I'm sure I'd said worse in my life.

Gigi turned back to Argenta. "I've almost got her running. Rewriting her directives without a manual has been a little tougher than I thought, but it will be worth it to have a warrior automaton at our side, instead of one who wants to do the laundry."

"Hey, will she respond to verbal commands? I don't want to have to rewrite her directives every time we need her to do something."

"Oh yes, automaidons are quite advanced. There's no way the upper crust would have it otherwise, would they? Heaven forbid some genteel lady learn how to do something so crass as automaton directivation."

There was a lot of bitter sarcasm in her voice but I didn't think just then was the time to get into it. "Can you set her to understand Anglic? I don't speak any Atlan."

Gigi looked away from the wires and switches inside Argenta's back and stared at me. "You don't speak Atlan? What backwater town do you come from?"

"It doesn't matter. Anglic, yes or no?"

"Of course," Gigi said, then reached in and turned a dial with a series of clicks. It was way too dark for me to see what she'd just done.

"What's the plan?" Gigi asked.

"Argenta creates a diversion, takes out Mister Shorty. You get into cold storage, find Eve, get her up and running. I'll sneak away in the confusion and get to the box to let out Serena. From there, we'll need to find weapons."

"None of them carry any firearms, luckily," Gigi said. She reached up and unscrewed Argenta's fake metal hair bun. Inside there was a switch. "Alright then. Could you crank the generator?"

There was a hand crank on the far side of the huge battery. I crawled over it and worked the crank. In the silence of the Booty Hold the whir of the generator sounded incredibly loud.

"Faster!" Gigi hissed from behind Argenta.

The faster I cranked the handle the louder the generator whirred.

"Who's back there?" Mister Shorty yelled. "Back to sleep!"

Like his yelling wouldn't wake up the dead. I cranked harder. Gigi threw the switch inside Argenta's hair bun.

The lights in Argenta's eyes flickered. She began to whir and click and emit the sound of gears moving against other gears as she sat up under her own power, straightening her head. Gigi held up a hand for me to stop cranking. I scrambled over the generator and looked in Argenta's glowing yellow eyes.

"Argenta, can you understand me?"

She nodded.

"Can you speak?"

She shook her head.

"Okay, listen. We are in a lot of trouble. This ship is controlled by pirates. Do you know what that means?'

Her brain box, which was mostly in her chest cavity, whirred and clicked and there might even have been a couple of muffled beeps, then she nodded.

"These pirates also happen to be slavers. We don't want to be slaves. So we need your help. Will you help us take over the ship?"

A lot more whirs and clicks and clanks and I definitely heard some beeps. She nodded.

I grinned at Gigi, who looked up from disconnecting the wires from Argenta's brain box and grinned back. "Awesome. Okay. My name is Sunset Val. She's Gigi. You only listen to us, okay?"

She nodded. Once Gigi finished screwing shut Argenta's back, the robot maid stood up. She had all the grace of a mechanical ballerina, sort of a jerky fluidity.

I led the way over the crates and boxes. "First things first. Mister Shorty."

Gigi, Argenta and I moved quickly. For all her jerky grace, Argenta utterly lacked any stealth. Metal shoes clanged loudly against the metal floor. It actually worked to our advantage, because Mister Shorty came looking for the source of the noise.

"Hear now, what's all this urk!"

Argenta grabbed him by the lapels and threw him against a pile of crates, swivelling at the waist. Mister Shorty struggled to his feet, but Gigi pounced on him and knocked his head against the floor a couple of times until the old man lay still.

"Is he dead?"

Gigi squeezed out her claws, a bloodthirsty look in her bright green cat eyes. "Do you want him dead?"

"No. He wasn't that bad. Compared to some of the others. Argenta, wrap him up in that carpet, okay?"

Argenta grabbed the carpet like it weighed nothing and with a flick unrolled it. Gigi and I dragged Mister Shorty by the arms over the carpet, then Argenta wrapped him in it. I hoped he wouldn't suffocate.

"Now what?" Gigi asked, dusting off her hands.

"Now you get to cold storage and wake up Eve. I'll get to Serena."

We nearly jumped out of our skins when a woman asked, "What you doing?"

I turned. It wasn't one of the female pirates, but one of the other slaves, one I hadn't really worked with before. She was big and heavy and looked tough, even wearing the same slave dress as the rest of us, even covered in the same filth and muck. Maybe because of all that. She looked like she'd known a life of hard work, not like a lot of the more genteel women who'd been taken as slaves. She reminded me of a trucker, or the way you'd imagine a woman trucker to be.

"We're taking the ship. We don't want to be slaves."

"They kill you. They kill us." Her Anglic was accented, but I understood her. "You not go."

Other women started to wake up. "Look, it's okay if you're scared. We're all scared. Gigi, you speak Atlan? Translate for me, okay?"

Gigi nodded, and repeated my words in Atlan.

"We're all scared because they've kept us scared. Beaten down. Worked us until we were exhausted. You think life as a slave will be any better? The pirates want to keep us pretty so that we sell for top price. That's why they don't beat us. But you think a slave's master is going to care what we look like once they've paid their price? If we don't take the ship, one day we'll look back and think this was easy."

Trucker sneered and said something in Atlan.

Gigi translated. "Taking the ship is impossible. We're not warriors."

I shook my head. "I'm not going to lie to you. It's not going to be a easy thing, taking on the pirates. They eat well, get lots of rest. They're used to a life of violence. But we outnumber them three to one! We can take them. I know we can. We just need to be brave and work together. I can be brave for you, if you'll be brave for me."

Gigi translated Trucker's words again. "This little girl wants to gets us all killed. We should stop her, wait here, and hope they don't kill us as punishment."

I went to Trucker. She was even bigger up close. "Don't you get it?! They won't kill us. We're too valuable as merchandise. We can use the element of surprise to overtake the first few before they raise the alarm. Argenta is strong, really strong. I have a friend, a patchwork, in cold storage. She's just as strong as any big muscle-bound man they've got. And I have a, a secret weapon." I didn't quite want to tell them about Serena just yet, just in case one of them ran to tell the pirates. "Trust me. I can make this happen. But only if you all help!"

A lot of the women were nodding now. Trucker saw which way the wind was blowing and frowned. She switched over to Anglic. "You get us killed."

"Maybe. But isn't it better to die free, than to live a slave?" I looked at all the other women. "In the morning they want to groom us. Turn us into pretty little slaves for market. They think we'll go along meekly, because that's what they expect of us. I say we take the ship, drop them all off at the nearest deserted island, and show them all what we're made of!"

The women got up, grinning fiercely. Some of the younger ones, anyway. Others looked terrified, but stood up anyway. Some of them stayed sitting on the floor, not looking anyone in the eyes. The ones who stood started going through boxes and crates, looking for things to use as weapons. Trucker glared at me, but turned to look for a weapon too. We found a crate filled with cast iron wrenches, some of which were big enough to use as clubs. I appropriated Mister Shorty's crowbar.

Gigi and Argenta disappeared while I organized the women. A few spoke Anglic well enough to translate for me. I told them to stay in the Booty Hold for fifteen minutes. If I wasn't back by then, they could go join Gigi and Argenta in cold storage.

"Where you go?" Trucker asked.

"To get our secret weapon."

"I go with you."

I thought about arguing for maybe a second and decided it wasn't worth the time or effort of getting her to understand that I moved quicker and quieter than she did. I just gave her a nod and headed up the metal stairs.

Looking back, I realize that it was definitely a good thing that our slave revolt happened in the middle of the night, without any planning. Okay, maybe a little planning would have been better, but on the whole it meant there was no chance that any of the crew had any idea of what was happening. They were really stupid and arrogant to put over two dozen women alone in a room with just one old guy to watch over them, an old guy whose interest lay not in guarding us but in accumulating wealth for his captain and himself.

We hurried along empty corridors, as fast as stealth would allow. Luckily the ship was pretty noisy, and our slippered feet against the metal floors kept us quiet. We heard the booted heels of a night watch pirate before we saw him, and hid. When he passed us, Trucker jumped out and smashed his head against the wall until he was unconscious. I didn't think that was such a great idea, but it was too late. We dragged him into nearby alcove, behind a ladder, and hoped he wouldn't wake up or be found by someone else. Under the blood covering his battered face, I recognized him as one of the men who had guarded the mess hall. I had a running tally of crew going in my head. My best bet was that there were about twenty pirates or so, including the captain, mate, and Dr. Enerva. Not a huge crew, which surprised me. I'd always thought pirates relied on greater numbers to take their prey. Anyway, with this guy and Mister Shorty out of the picture, that only meant about eighteen or so to go. I hoped.

I'd been to the box and back a couple of times, so I had a pretty good idea how to get there. We only got sidetracked twice, eating up precious seconds, but eventually I found the right stairwell down to the hallway that led to the boxes.

Considering how painfully I'd been blinded by the lone light in the corridor when I'd been hauled out by Karl, it surprised me to find the corridor quite dim compared to the rest of the ship. We found Serena's box easily enough. It was the only one that was locked.

"Serena!"

"Who is it?"

"It's me, Val! I'm here to get you out."

"I am ready, Wal."

I looked at the huge padlock on the door. It made me wonder how Karl had opened my box. Where did he get the key? There wasn't a convenient hook on the wall nearby, and boxed prisoners didn't require jailers or guards. We looked for a key for maybe a minute, then I told Trucker to look out for more night watch as I set about getting the padlock off with Mister Shorty's crowbar.

Two hits was all it took for me to slip and gash open my already injured hand with the crowbar. The noise was horrendously loud, and now I couldn't hold the crowbar. Way to go, Val.

Trucker tsked behind me and grabbed the crowbar from my hands. She stuck it through the loop on the padlock, then put her foot on the crowbar and leaned on it. When she was satisfied it would hold her weight, she sort of jumped a little on it. The lock held firm. Using one hand to balance on the crowbar, she stood up on it, putting her full and not inconsiderable weight on it. Then she bounced once on the bar.

The lock shattered as the metal loop strained and twisted under her weight. The crowbar clattered to the metal floor. Trucker nearly took a spill too, but I caught her with a grin. She shook her head disapprovingly at me.

I went to Serena's box. "Close your eyes, it's bright out here."

"Ready."

I opened the door, noting absently that its inside face had been dented somehow. Within the box itself, Serena lay curled up, long limbs folded beneath her slender body, eyes shut against the relative brightness of the corridor outside the box. Her pale skin and long, pale hair combined with the starkness of the shadows to make it seem like somehow the world inside Serena's box was an old black and white movie. Not thinking, I reached in to help her out and the filthiness of my hand and the redness of the bleeding gash brought colour back into my field of vision.

Serena's eyes snapped open, cold and bright blue and locked onto the blood in my palm. Her full lips went slack as her jaw widened with hunger, and I saw the glitter of her incisors, longer than any human's had ever been.

I offered her my hand. "Take it. We need you. Just... don't drink me dry, okay?"

"Vampyri?!" Trucker yelled. "This secret weapon?!"

"Shut up! We need her." I turned back to Serena, keeping my eyes on hers even as she kept hers on my palm. "Serena, take it. Drink my blood."

She ran a dry tongue over those full, parched lips. Her eyes went to my face, saw my offer was honest, and took it.

At first it kind of tickled, feeling her tongue flicker across my palm. I might have flinched a little, because she grabbed my wrist and pressed her mouth against the gash. That's when it stopped tickling.

It didn't hurt, exactly. Just a very uncomfortable feeling, as she sucked at the wound, my wrist caught in her iron grip. After a couple of seconds my hand kind of went numb. Probably some kind of anaesthetic in her saliva. Maybe even an anticoagulant, like vampire bats and mosquitoes, thank you very much Discovery channel.

My every movement brought immediate, harsh correction from her, holding my wounded hand at exactly the right angle to maximize the bleeding. I felt kind of sick to my stomach, but I forced myself to watch.

It felt like forever but couldn't have been more than a couple of minutes before she forced my hand away from her hunger. "Enough! No more."

"You haven't eaten in days." When had I sunk to my knees? Why was I so lightheaded? Oh, right, I'd just fed a vampire from my own private reserve.

"I have taken enough to get us past our first obstacle," she said, crawling out of the box, my blood smeared on her lips and chin. Serena was so much taller standing up. Trucker kept the crowbar between her and the vampyri.

Serena said something to her in Atlan, rapid and harsh, a voice used to command. Trucker answered back, her fear surrendering what little authority she had. They talked for a little bit, then Serena offered me her hand. I took it, careful to keep my bloody hand away from her, out of sight, just in case she lost control and sucked me dry.

"Show me the pirate you attacked on the vay here," Serena said to me, holding me up with one arm propped under my armpits.

"I can walk."

"Do not argue, Sunset Wal. Now is not the time for false pride. You are veakened from my feeding, this I know. Your blood, it is different from any I have ever tasted. Ve vill talk on this more, once ve have taken the ship."

She held me up and I showed her the way, Trucker following behind. When we got to the spot where we'd hidden the unconscious night patrol pirate, Serena handed me off to Trucker and said something in Atlan. Trucker spat back something angry. Serena just raised an eyebrow at her and said nothing. Trucker held her look for a second or two, then looked away.

"He's over there."

"I can smell him, Sunset Wal. Vait here."

She disappeared into the shadows of the alcove. After a couple of minutes, she came back out, her chin and shirt drenched with blood.

"Is he dead?"

She wiped her forearm across her bloody face. "You are upset by this?"

I thought about it, wasting even more time. "I don't know."

"There vill be deaths this night, Sunset Wal. Best harden yourself to vhat lies ahead."

"Yeah. Okay." I took a deep breath. "Do you still need to feed?"

"No. My hunger is sated. For now."

"Okay. So, we need weapons."

"Pirates keep their veapons locked away, to prevent any ideas of mutiny. Only on the attack does the captain allow the mate to open the veapons locker."

"Great. So no one has any weapons."

"Unless of course someone raises the alarm."

"Free other women," Trucker said, the first thing she'd said to me since we freed Serena.

"Yeah, I know," I said, heading back toward the Booty Hold.

Trucker shook her head. "No. Free others. From room."

"Oh. Good idea. Okay, let's do that."

"You do not vish to get some veapons first?"

"Once we free the other women, you and I will get to the weapons locker. Trucker can bring them to the Booty Hold or cold storage or wherever the others are."

"Who?"

"Who?"

"Oh, sorry. What's your name?"

Trucker looked at me. "Surla."

"I'm Sunset Val and this is Serena Heartlace. Once we free the women from the slave quarters, you lead them to the Booty Hold. Serena and I will get weapons from the weapons locker and meet you there."

"Better bring women to locker. Better not... make two. Stay one."

"You don't want to split up."

"No."

Serena watched me, judging me. I could feel her waiting to see how I'd handle this.

"Surla. When this is over, we can argue about who gets to do what. Right now, Serena and I are the only ones with a plan. If we argue over every little thing, we are going to lose the element of surprise. We're going to get caught. We're going to be sold as slaves. Assuming they don't just kill us for causing so much trouble. So. Please. Stop arguing with me and do what you're told!"

From the set of her jaw I knew she wanted to argue, but also realized that I was right, and it pissed her off. I just glared at her. Serena stayed so still she could have been a sculpture.

Finally Surla nodded and looked away. She turned and headed down towards the slave quarters. Only once she was a little ahead of us did I let out a sigh of relief.

"Good," Serena said from right beside me. She was so quiet I actually jumped. "You vill make excellent captain, Sunset Wal."

"Captain? Me?"

She just grinned at me and moved ahead, silent and stealthy as a panther on the prowl.

I hadn't thought of it. Me, as captain. It had a nice ring to it. Captain Sunset Val.

But thinking that far ahead was pretty silly. We could be discovered at any moment. We could be killed. Thinking further than the next few minutes was just daydreaming. Anything beyond getting to the weapons locker, which I had no idea where it was, and getting ourselves some arms, which I had no idea if I'd be able to use, was silly.

One thing at a time.

Serena led the way like she knew where she was going. Up stairs and down corridors, pausing to check around corners before plunging ahead. I kept up as best I could. I was still a little lightheaded, and she was fast. Crazy fast. Sometimes I'd turn a corner and she'd already be all the way down the corridor, checking the next corner and waving me forward.

We wound up on the deck with the rugs and paintings and wooden doors. Through one door we heard snoring. Through another we heard the sounds of a very different kind of nocturnal activity. I felt my face heat up as I blushed from embarrassment. Serena smiled a predatory smile. She leaned in close to my ear.

"This is perfect. They vill be too preoccupied to vant to investigate any noises, and the rest of the crew vill assume it to be them."

"Yeah, they are going at it pretty loudly."

"Who is it, do you know?"

I thought I recognized Dr. Enerva's voice. "Probably the doctor and the first mate."

"Excellent! The veapons locker vill be close by. Only the mate and the captain vill have the key."

We checked a couple of doors, then found one that was locked. Serena grabbed the doorknob in both hand and twisted. At first nothing happened. Serena's full lips pressed together in a thin line of determination. Tendons stood out in her neck and wrists as she forced. Her pale knuckles paled even whiter. Her arms shook with the effort. Then, with a sudden snap, the doorknob turned and the door opened.

Past the door was a small closet, just big enough to walk into. A number of swords hung by belted scabbards on a rack. A series of shelves held pistols. A couple of rifles were propped up in the corner.

Serena trailed a finger along the swords, quickly flipping through them like a shopaholic looking through a bargain rack. She took a couple out of the scabbard.

"You know the sword?"

"I've fenced with epee and foil. Epee is better."

"Agreed. Your size and frame are better suited to epee. Take this."

She handed me a sword. It wasn't much to look at, but it was really well balanced. I took it out of the scabbard and gave it a couple of passes. It would do. I strapped the belt around me, cinching it tight.

Serena had already chosen her weapon and strapped it on. Then she grabbed what looked like a messenger bag from one of the shelves and handed it to me.

"Take as many of the pistols as you can carry. I vill take the swords."

I looked at the pistols and grabbed one. It was the first time I'd ever held a gun, and I was surprised at how heavy it was. I took a deep breath, fighting off the urge to cry or scream or both. "This is it, isn't it? People are going to die now."

Serena looked at me, one arm full of swords. She put the other hand on my shoulder. "Yes, Sunset Wal. People vill die. But many more people vill die if ve do not stop these pirates, these slavers." From her, it was a curse word. "Not every voman taken vinds up in a noble's house as a serving girl. Most go to the manufactories. Some find themselves sold to the pleasure houses. Neither fate is wery pleasant."

I asked, "Why aren't any men taken as slaves?"

"Men are too much trouble. From their military training, yes? Two years every man gives to the empire. It makes them unlikely to be easily taken, too difficult to break. Vomen are seen as easier to cow into submission. Little did they expect you. Besides, in many places it is illegal to take men as slaves. The only male slaves allowed in these places are those born to female slaves."

"That is totally sexist!"

Serena snorted a laugh. "Velcome to the vorld, Sunset Wal. It is sexist and racist and unfair."

"This sucks. Okay, I'm pissed off now."

"Vhat this means?"

"Pissed off? Really angry."

"Ah. And you vere not 'pissed off' before?"

"Not this pissed off, no."

"So the killing, it can begin?"

She wasn't bloodthirsty about it. It was just a matter of fact, for her.

I nodded. It was a matter of fact for me, too. It had to be. People would die, because I said it was time for them to die. I told myself to suck it up and deal with it later. "Yeah. Go time."

I filled the satchel with as many pistols as I could carry, including a two-gun belt I cinched around my waist. I'd never used a gun but if we couldn't take all of them I wanted to make sure I had a couple, just in case. Serena had most of the swords looped over her shoulders and tucked under one arm. She held one of the finer swords drawn and ready in her free hand.

"Go time," she said, grinning at me wide enough for me to see her fangs.

I stumbled at first under the weight of the gun satchel, but I swung it around behind me and leaned into the burden. Serena led the way, much slower this time. Luckily the last couple of weeks had gotten me used to hard work and exercise. With the satchel behind me I managed a pretty decently paced waddle.

We got to the Booty Hold just in time for the alarm to go off.

Chapter Seventeen

Go Time

Not only was the klaxon incredibly loud as it echoed through the Booty Hold, but the Booty Hold was completely dark. The only illumination came from the flashing red alarm light, giving bloody glimpses of the room. From what I could see in the after-images left on my retinas, the Booty Hold was empty.

Which is to say, it still had all the stuff, the treasure, the booty the pirates had taken, piled into Mister Shorty's neat and organized piles, but all the women were gone. I even spotted Mister Shorty still rolled up in his carpet as I scanned the room frantically.

Then I realized. "Cold storage!"

Serena jumped at the sound of my shout, jolted out of me by the force of memory finally overpowering panic. I ran for the far end of the Booty Hold. Well, I waddled as fast as I could with the weight of the gun satchel heavy on my back. Serena followed, her head scanning back and forth as she watched for any hint of the pirates' presence, alert for any attack or ambush in the area.

Definitely starting to freak, I made it to the room that served as the cold storage. I opened the huge, double wide, double high door, hauling on it with both hands, and a wave of cold air passed over me. Something metallic moved towards us.

"Argenta halt!"

Gigi came running out of the cold storage room, waving her hands. Argenta had halted right in the middle of a punch aimed at Serena's head. I noticed Serena had raised her sword to block the blow. Talk about reflexes. I had barely had a chance to see what had come out of the room.

"This is your secret weapon?" Gigi asked me.

"Yeah. Serena, this is Gigi and Argenta."

Gigi turned to the automaidon. "Argenta, identify friend."

Argenta lowered her arm, turned to Gigi and nodded.

"Did you get Eve?"

"Y-y-y-yes, Mmmmiss."

Eve stumbled out of the cold storage room on stiff legs, shivering and blue with cold. There were bright white patches on her skin, like freezer burn. It surprised me how glad I was to see her. The other women followed after her, all shivering. Serena started handing out swords and guns.

"Sorry about the lights," Gigi said. "Something blew when we woke Eve up."

I went to Eve and put my hand on her arm. It was like touching a ham in a freezer, frozen solid. I smiled up at her.

"We've got to get you warmed up."

"I sh-sh-sh-all b-b-be fffffine, Mmmmmisssss."

"No arguments, okay? Besides, I have a job for you. Gigi, you and Eve take a dozen women and go shut down the engines, okay?"

Gigi grinned. "Okay!"

"Mmmmissss?"

"Eve, it's warmer there than anywhere on the ship, and you'll thaw out faster. Plus, you know engines, am I right?"

"Yyyyes, Mmmiss."

"Okay then. You help Gigi." She seemed a little slower than I remembered, like her brain had frozen, too. I hoped her stay in cold storage hadn't damaged anything. Or at least, anything a patchwork couldn't fix.

There was noise from the entrance to the Booty Hold and I pulled out my sword. Freed of the scabbard it was even better balanced. Serena's choice suited me perfectly. The other women fumbled with their swords and guns as we faced whatever was coming for us.

Which, luckily, turned out to be Surla and the other slaves. I let out a phew of relief.

"Give them whatever weapons are left," I told the women. "Argenta, you stay with me, okay?"

The robot nodded.

"Okay, Gigi needs volunteers to shut down the engines. Which probably means kicking Luke's sorry ass. Anyone interested?"

Seems quite a few women had felt the flat of Luke's shovel, because we had more volunteers than we needed. I picked out a dozen or so, including Surla, and sent them with Gigi and Eve.

"Vhere are ve going?"

"We need to take the ship, so, where would the wheel be?"

"The vheelhouse, of course."

"Don't act like everyone knows that."

With a nod, I let Serena take the lead. She knew ships, I'll give her that. She had the layout figured out just from the corridors we'd moved through, making her way forward with a confidence I utterly lacked. Not that I showed it, of course. The other women hadn't been raised to believe that mere females could do this sort of thing. I would show them the errors in that kind of thinking.

We ran into a search party of pirates I didn't recognize, dressed in their nightshirts and hastily donned boots. They were all lean, mean, pirating machines, armed with whatever Serena and I had left behind in the weapons locker. A couple of them had long knives, probably snatched from the kitchen.

Serena lay into them like a dancer, twisting and dodging and striking with the kind of finesse I could only dream about achieving. The clatter of blade on blade filled the corridor, ringing and echoing. Serena very nearly took them all on by herself, but there were too many. One of them got past her dance of death and came right at me, sword raised.

It wasn't like on the practice mat, or even at competition. For one thing, I'd never fought in such close quarters before, even more narrow than a fencing piste. The walls were so close there was barely enough room for me to swing my sword from side to side, and the ceiling had all kinds of pipes and cables suspended from it. For another, this guy had no rules, no style. His only goal was to put the sharp end of his sword into my guts, and it was three or four passes before I was able to do more than block his single-minded, desperate attacks. I got him off balance with a parry and riposted, lunging forward. My instincts honed by months of training paid off well, and I drew back from the attack.

Which turned out to be a pretty stupid thing to do, since he was trying to kill me and I just stopped my blade from plunging into his chest. It would have been a perfect hit, too.

He looked at me with confusion pure and clear on his face, then shook his head as if he couldn't believe either his luck or my stupidity.

Argenta rushed past me and grabbed his raised sword arm with one robotic hand, then planted the other square in his face. I watched teeth fly and clatter against the wall. Then Serena's blade sprouted from the middle of his chest and he stared at it, stunned. She twisted and pulled and her sword schlocked out of his back with a gout of blood.

"No time for toying vith them, Sunset Wal! Kill and be done!"

I didn't answer. I concentrated on not throwing up. Serena stood in a circle of twitching bodies. Some of them moaned, and she jabbed them with her sword. The moaning stopped.

She'd killed five pirates while I learned that competitive fencing isn't the same as swordplay. For a dark, terrible second, I didn't think I could go on. I just wanted to curl up in a ball and let them sell me into slavery. Put me in a factory or whatever. At least then I wouldn't have to be responsible for any more deaths.

Serena came to me, put a hand on my shoulder. Glanced behind me, at the other women there. I turned.

Some of them were crying. Some of them were fiercely grinning. Most of them looked horrified at what Serena, Argenta and I had just done.

"Be brave for them," Serena said, her voice pitched low to keep her words for my ears alone. "And they vill be brave for you."

I looked at her. Smiled a grim smile with no humour in it. Turned back to the other women.

"Come on, ladies. They've taken our lives from us. Now let's take their ship from them."

I told Argenta to lead the way up the stairwell, just in case we'd left any of the pistols behind. Our slave revolt would have gotten off to a pretty depressing start if one of us took a bullet in the head while climbing a staircase or ladder.

Argenta went first up the stairs, peeking her head into the upper level to look around before continuing. We followed, abandoning silence in favour of speed. We needed to get to the wheelhouse.

We were one deck below the deck with the carpeted floors and paintings on the walls, and Serena continued to head forward. I'd seen enough movies about pirates to think I knew something about ships, because I grabbed her arm to slow her down for a second.

"You sure the wheel isn't on the topmost deck? Like, outside?"

"Vhy vould the vheel be outside?"

"So the driver can see where he's going?"

Understanding dawned on her pale face. Traces of blood still darkened her lips and chin. "Ah, on a sailing ship, yes. On an airship, no. This vay."

She led us to a set of double wooden doors, grabbed a handle and pulled.

It didn't budge. She pushed, again to no effect. She handed me her sword and grabbed the handle with both hands. The door wouldn't move.

"Argenta, help her."

The automaidon stepped up and she and Serena tried to get the doors open. I was just about to tell them to kick it in when there were screams from the back of our group. I looked but couldn't see through all the women in the way.

"Argenta, get those doors open!" I tossed Serena her sword and turned to the crowd of women. "Look out! Coming through! Make way!"

Serena and I forced our way through the women. Some of them got out of the way. Some of them I had to push out of the way. Some of them were actively trying to move in the opposite direction we were going.

"MAKE VAY!"

The women crushed themselves against the walls of the corridor to get out of our way. About halfway through the crowd of women, I saw why they'd been screaming. We'd been found by the crew.

Dreads and Diana led a group of their shipmates, grabbing women and tying ropes around their wrists and throats. Dreads disarmed them, Diana roped them, the other crew held them.

Some of our women fought. Some just gave up.

"ATTACK!" Serena bellowed. "ATTACK! ATTACK! ATTACK!"

"Come on girls, we can do this!" I didn't need to say anything, since they'd already begun to follow Serena's order, but I kind of felt I had to. Serena might have scared the ones who weren't doing anything into attacking, but I wanted to encourage the ones who were already fighting.

It stunned me, how unprepared the pirates were for us to rise up and rebel. Once the screaming stopped and the counter attack began, a couple of the pirates just stood there, astonished. One guy just watched, mouth gaping open, as four women jumped him, pounding and pummelling him with wrenches and pipes, slashing and hacking at him with swords.

Their stunned amazement didn't last long. Dreads recovered especially quickly. His disarming manoeuvres changed to disabling attacks, slaps and trips and twists designed to take an opponent out, preferably without permanent damage.

I pointed with my sword. "Serena! Dreads! Go!"

She sheathed her sword and pounced, leaping right over the women and pirates crowding the corridor, and landed right next to him. Her pale skin, pale hair, and pale but filthy smock were a stark contrast to his dark skin, dark dreadlocks and fine black leather clothes. She faced her unarmed opponent with open hands.

He grinned and attacked.

I would have loved to watch, but right about then two things happened. The first was, Diana grabbed me by my hair.

"You!" she spat, doing some kind of nerve pinch in my elbow that made me cry out in pain and drop my sword. "You've been nothing but trouble since we took you on board!"

"How can you do this to other women?!" I asked. "What's wrong with you?"

My questions startled her. She stared at me, confused. "What does our gender have anything to do with anything?"

That caught me off guard. Our shared gender didn't have anything to do with it, not really, I supposed. It just seemed wrong to me that a woman would be involved with the sale of other women into slavery. "You're a bitch."

"I'll take that as a compliment," she answered, then looped some rope over my head and around my throat.

Remember I said two things happened just then? Well, the second thing happened. Argenta showed up, pointing back at the doors she'd ripped off their hinges.

"Argenta, get her off me!" The rope around my throat made it hard for me to speak, and I wasn't sure Argenta heard me over the screams and yells and dull thuds of iron against flesh.

I needn't have worried, though. Her hearing sensors were a lot better than a normal human's. She reached out and grabbed Diana by the wrist, yanked her past me and slammed her into the wall. Diana was knocked out immediately. Then Argenta helped me up, taking the rope off of my throat.

"Thanks, Argenta, good job."

I checked out our situation. Serena had taken out Dreads. Diana was out for the count. The other pirates had been subdued by the overwhelming number of women.

Some of the women were hurt, though. Nothing serious, just some sprains and bruises, but a couple probably had broken bones. Obviously when the pirates had seen it was going badly for them, they changed their attacks, no longer afraid of damaging the merchandise in favour of saving their own skins.

Only a couple of pirates had occupied the wheelhouse, and they had attacked Argenta when she'd torn open the doors. Which pretty much tells you how smart they were. Her self-defence programming had kicked in and she'd knocked them out. Or killed them, it was kind of hard to tell, and I didn't have time to check.

We left the injured women in the wheelhouse. One of the women had been a nurse before she'd been captured, so I left the injured women in her care.

Using their own rope against them, we tied up the four surviving pirates. Five of the others were dead. Many of the women had lost husbands and boyfriends, brothers and fathers, during the attacks that had taken them prisoners and slaves. Revenge against their murderers had seemed hopeless until I gave them that hope. That's me, right? Bringer of homicidal hope.

"We have the wheelhouse. Now what?"

Serena looked at me. Her face was so grim it was practically a snarl. "Now ve find the captain and kill him."

"Right." I picked out a dozen women who still looked hungry for revenge and left the rest to guard the wheelhouse. "Come on girls, there's still plenty of killing to do."

Chapter Eighteen

One Scrape Costs An Arm And a Leg

We left the wheelhouse. I heard sounds of fighting coming from down below somewhere. That's when I realized I couldn't hear or feel the rhythmic pounding of the engines. Gigi and Eve must have captured the engine rooms and shut down the boilers. Those sounds of fighting were them desperately fending off a wave of attacking pirates, who very obviously didn't care about the state of the merchandise. I learned all this later, but their backup plan was to sell our parts to a patchwork factory and recoup at least a little of the cost of their investment. Nice guys.

My heart said to charge to their rescue to help Gigi and Eve, two of the only friends I had in this world. My head said to stay in the game, keep focused, find the captain and formally take command of the ship. If I'd listened to my heart I might have been spared some nightmares later on.

We moved through the ship, alert to any possible threat. We saw no one.

We found the surgeon's quarters. Serena opened the door, sniffed once, then coughed and gagged.

I felt my blood run cold. Whatever made a vampyri sick had to be pretty hellish. I pulled out one of my pistols and held it in front of me, hoping the sight of it would deter any potential attackers.

I entered the room. I couldn't smell anything other than the stench of rotting meat. Serena's sense of smell must have been more sensitive than mine. There were a couple of beds with bloodstained sheets, and the metal floor seemed permanently stained with blood. Along one wall were shelves covered with glass jars of all sizes and shapes, filled with body parts floating in some amber fluid. I could swear the jar of eyeballs was looking at me as I passed.

In one corner was a pile of blood-soaked meaty parts that had seen better days, obviously the source of the stench. A cloud of flies buzzed sickeningly around the pile.

At the back of the room was a table. On the table, covered by a sheet, lay the girl who'd gashed her shin on the stairs and been sent here. From the rise and fall of the sheet covering her chest, I knew she slept peacefully. I went to wake her.

As I drew closer I began to suspect something was wrong. The far side of her face was covered in a bloody cloth. Her far arm and leg were oddly misshapen under the sheet.

The urge to vomit loomed. "Oh god," I said.

I tried, but I couldn't stop myself. I reached out and pulled the bloody cloth away from her face. It came away with a sickening sucking noise, heavy with the weight of blood seeped out and soaked up.

Under it, the girl's eye had been removed, replaced with a glass lens. Blood and pus seeped from the red, swollen skin around the replacement. Part of her hair had been shaved away, and a grotesque distended scar ran from her new eye, over her ear, to the back of her head.

I pulled down the sheet. Her privates were covered for propriety's sake with bloodstained under-things, but she was otherwise unclothed. Straps kept her secured to the table. Her right arm above the shoulder and right leg just below the hip had been replaced with metal ones of rough robotic design. Pistons and tubes were clearly visible running the length of her new limbs. Bolts held the prosthetics securely in place, attached through her skin, sinking into the bone beneath.

The lensed eye shuttered open and closed, like an old-fashioned non-digital camera lens. Then her normal eyelid flickered open, and she said something in Atlan.

"Sorry, no habla. Anglic?"

"Please. Kill me," she whispered, glancing at the gun in my hand.

"What?"

She reached out to grab my wrist, just barely stopped by the straps holding her down. "Please. The pain. Things she do. Too much. Kill me."

I put the gun back in my holster. "No way."

"I not live like this."

"Don't say that!" I snapped at her, loosening her bonds. "Lots of people have it a lot worse than you! Suicide is not the answer!"

"What is?"

"Revenge!" It just sort of popped out of my mouth before I thought about it. I know, I know, a person seeking revenge needs to dig two graves, one for their target and one for themselves. I read that somewhere. But better she should live through today than ask me to help her suicide herself. Sometimes, the only thing you've got to live for is getting to the end of the day.

She needed help sitting up, not used to the weight of her new limbs. "Revenge?"

"Revenge. Kill the evil bitch that did this to you!"

She raised her replacement arm, clenching the skeletal metal fingers into a fist with the grind of gears and the hiss of pistons. A tear spilled down her cheek from her remaining natural eye.

"Come with me, and I promise you'll get a chance to kill her."

"Kill. Yes. Kill her."

Serena poked her head into the room, one hand over her nose and mouth. "Sunset Wal, ve must go!"

I turned back to the girl. "Can you walk?"

"Yes. She make me. Much pain. I kill her."

She limped forward slowly, grimacing against the pain.

"Hang on." I grabbed the sheet and wrapped it around her like she was going to a toga party. It wasn't much, but I figured she'd rather have something on than go running around in blood-soaked underwear.

"Thank you," she said.

"I'm Sunset Val. What's your name?"

"Molly Wolfwood."

"Come on, Molly. We've got some killing to do."

"Yes. Kill. Kill."

She was freaking me out a little with the whole "Kill, kill" thing, but whatever. As long as she wasn't killing herself, I could manage her murderous muttering.

The other women looked horrified when we came out of the surgeon's quarters. Some even stepped back from Molly, hands covering their mouths in horror. Molly didn't notice. She just kept on whispering "Kill. Kill her. Kill!" over and over. Unfortunately unsettling, unless inhuman, like Serena. The vampyri vixen approved of vengeance.

Okay, okay, I'll try to control the alliteration. Anyway.

We made our way as quickly as Molly's limping would allow, finally coming to the hangar bay. A group of pirates were strapping themselves into the ornithopters, including Tyr Ebonfury and Dr. Enerva.

"KILL HER!" Molly shrieked, hobbling forward.

The pirates who hadn't yet strapped in rushed at us, weapons raised. I didn't wonder how they'd gotten weapons. I didn't have time. A pirate I didn't recognize was in front of me, sword raised for a killing blow. I parried his first attack and danced away from his second, then it was all thrusts and parries, ripostes and recovers. Unlike the first pirate I'd fought, this guy knew his way around a sword. My world contracted to the clatter of my blade against his. Dimly I knew that Serena and Tyr were fighting, that Molly had used her mechanical arm as a club against a couple of pirates, that the other women were swarming over the ornithopters and killing the pilots with a frightening fury. There were screams and howls and moans. Women were dying. Pirates were dying. All around me.

And all I saw was his flashing blade. All I heard was the clash of steel. My heart was pounding. My breath came in gasps. He got lucky, darting past my block to slash along my left side. My ribs erupted in fire, pain adding a new focus to our engagement. I pressed my elbow into my side to hopefully slow the bleeding.

I finally had my opening in his defence, and I took it. My blade sank six inches into his stomach. He gasped. I pulled on my sword to remove it but it held firm, trapped in the suction of the wound. He raised his sword to finish me off, a dying act of revenge. I tried pushing on the blade to loosen it but it just sank in further. He moaned and swung his sword at me. I ducked under the attack, too close for his longer reach. Grateful for my small size, I pressed a foot into his stomach and heaved on the sword, twisting it as I pulled. Finally it came free, bloody halfway to the hilt. He staggered back into a lever, tripped and fell.

The lever, it turned out, opened the launch doors in the hangar floor. Three pirates and two women fell screaming to their deaths before the others managed to run away and jump clear.

A scream pierced the howl of wind and clamour of battle, followed by a sharp loud crack. I turned and saw Dr. Enerva training a small revolver on Molly. Molly had her mechanical arm held in front of her like a shield. She adapted quickly, I'll give her that.

Tyr turned from his fight with Serena and saw his beloved in peril. Serena was more than happy to take the opening, and she stabbed him in the shoulder. He let out a grunt of pain and really let her have it, a torrent of attacks designed not to display any prowess but rather to shatter an opponent's reserve, to strike terror. Hey, I was terrified, and it wasn't me he was fighting.

One of the ornithopters took fight and escaped out the launch doors. Dimly I recognized Creedance aboard the orny, and a tiny bloom of relief burst in my heart. He had been pretty decent to me, and it made me glad that he had managed to escape.

One of Tyr's blows finally shattered Serena's sword. Left holding a hilt with three inches of blade sticking out, cornered against the wall, Serena readied herself for his killing blow.

It never came. Once Serena was disarmed, Tyr turned and ran for Enerva. She'd fired again and again, but Molly wouldn't be denied her revenge by mere bullets.

Tyr slashed the back of Molly's good leg, just above the knee. She fell with a scream of pain. He jumped into the ornithopter and started up the engine. I ran toward them, determined to stop them from escaping our justice.

Too late. The wings spread out, beating faster and faster until the vehicle took to the air and fled through the launch doors into the night sky.

"Dammit!" I screamed.

"Kill. Kill." Molly panted, curled on her natural side.

I pulled off my sword belt and cinched it around her thigh, a simple tourniquet I hoped would keep her from bleeding to death, liked I'd been taught in CPR. "Yes, you will. Stay alive and I swear we will hunt her down."

She glanced at me, tears of pain and frustration streaming down her face. She nodded, once, then wept.

Serena came up behind me. "Ve must find the captain, Sunset Wal."

I turned to her just in time to see her clench up, every muscle flexing, her face a grotesque grimace of pain. She fell to the floor, unconscious.

"You've found him, I think," Captain Crow said, holding his electric walking stick in one bony hand, up in front of him, like a sword.

I grabbed my sword and stood up.

"You and your sorry crew will pay for the damages you've cost me," Captain Crow snarled. The wind from the open launch doors flapped his black coat and blacker cloak around him like the tattered rags of a scarecrow, or the wings of his namesake.

I glared at him. "Yeah, yeah, whatever. En garde, you sack of bones."

Chapter Nineteen

The End of My Life As a Slave

Over his shoulder behind him I saw Argenta lying in a heap. He must have zapped her with his stick, too. Some of the women were tying up the remaining pirates. Others were wrapping up their own wounds. A few just sat where they were, weeping with relief or long unshed tears of grief. No one was going to help me.

The pirates were defeated. That much I knew for sure. If he killed me, I'd go to my grave knowing I'd done something of worth in this weirdo world. Serena could take command. If she woke up.

Sparks of electricity arced across my blade as I blocked his blow. Somehow the charge was not channelled to me, for which I was immediately grateful. I spent several moments just blocking his attacks, parrying without riposting, making sure that I wasn't grounded and that first pass hadn't been a fluke.

It wasn't. Something in the hilt, maybe, was keeping me from being zapped along my own sword. Of course, if he touched me directly, that would be a different story. I had to make sure that didn't happen. With the open launch doors to my left promising a long drop and a sudden stop, I had to get clear, give myself some room to move.

Captain Crow's features were set in a permanent snarl. "You'll pay, oh yes, I swear you'll pay!"

"So you said. Will you take a check?" I dodged a slash, parried another, riposted a third.

"Do you know what you've done?" He lunged, blocked a slash of mine, retreated in front of another.

"Educate me." I riposted.

"The world feared the dreaded Captain Crow. Greatest slaver in the world!" He slashed at my head. I ducked. He slashed and lunged again. I parried, his stick sparking with electricity.

"Slavery is wrong!" I answered. He parried my advance, I parried his. He recovered just as I tried an encirclement.

He ignored me. "People knew, if I took them a slave, they'd be well treated until sold. No beatings! No starvation!" His slashes grew more animated with his rage. Slash followed slash, and it was all I could do to dodge and parry his attacks. Then in the midst of all the wild slashing and the clatter of walking stick on blade, he actually tried a prise de fer!

"Yeah, you're a great guy." I recovered, barely, retreating and parrying.

He advanced on me, lunging and slashing. "Didn't need a tremendous crew! Better shares of the profits! Everybody happy!" His cane whirled before me in an envelopment.

I kept retreating and parrying. "Except the slaves maybe?"

"Now it'll be fights all the time! No surrenders! A rebellion? Slaves unhappy? More crew! Less profit!" His sword style was so impossible to judge, all wild hacking and slashing and lunging, and then suddenly out of nowhere a textbook example of a more civilized manoeuvre. His chin was covered with spit. Sweat poured down his face. His long black hair had come loose and whipped about in the wind. His eyes were wide with rage. Yeah, he and reason had pretty much totally broken up and gone their separate ways.

He had no hilt on his cane, no foible to catch with my sword. I stepped into his range, sliding my blade along the stick. I forced his arm up, using both hands on my hilt.

I looked up into his eyes, which were bright with madness. "You're an evil son of a bitch!"

He sneered down at me. "You'll live a long unhappy life as my personal slave."

I leapt back, letting him bring the stick down. I used the prise de fer against him, disarming him, slashing his wrist with the tip of my blade. He stared at his own hand, shocked.

This time my training didn't stop me from doing what needed to be done. I lunged forward and ran him through with my sword. He stumbled back, pulling the hilt from my grasp. He looked at the blade protruding from his chest, confused. His eyes rolled back in his head and he pitched backward.

Out the open launch doors.

The captain was dead. The ship was ours.

I sank to my knees, exhausted and grateful.

Chapter Twenty

Spoiling Ourselves

First things had to be first. Celebrations would come later.

We locked up the remaining pirates in the former slave quarters. There were only about seven of them, including Diana and Dreads. Nine pirates were dead, including the captain, that dark-haired female pirate who was the only other woman besides Diana in their crew, and Luke. The few that remained escaped in the ornithopters. We'd figure out what to do about the captured pirates when we had the time. The dead pirates we dumped overboard with no ceremony whatsoever. The seventeen dead women, almost half our number, we bundled into blankets. Surla was one of them. An older woman said something that sounded like a prayer, and then they sang a hymn or something, all in Atlan so I couldn't understand a word. Then we dumped their bodies, too.

I ordered a ship-wide search to make sure there were no pirates hiding out, waiting for a time to seek revenge on us. That took a while, mostly because I didn't speak any Atlan. Molly was a big help, translating for me. Once we hooked up again with Gigi and Eve, it went easier. Eve and a couple of the women helped patch up our wounded. She even tore up her sleeves to make bandages when the ones from the surgeon's room ran out. No one knew her way around a needle and thread like Eve. She cleaned and closed the cut on my ribs with expert ease. Some of the women, the ones who weren't with Gigi and Eve, didn't know what to make of the tall, scarred girl, but the ones who'd taken the engine room considered her some kind of hero. I promised myself I'd get the story out of her later. Argenta helped me put Serena somewhere sunproof. Anywhere but the box again. One of the crew cabins didn't have a porthole, so we stuck her in there.

Dawn came while we searched the ship. From the wheelhouse, I watched the sky lighten, then the sudden, almost unexpected brilliance of the sun appearing over the ocean horizon. It was more glorious than anything I had ever seen.

During our search we found the ship's laundry room, a hot steamy room over the engines, near the box. We washed ourselves off in there, clearing away blood and sweat and grime. A mirror in one of the crew's quarters had told me what I never wanted to know, namely, how filthy I was. My skin was nearly black from coal dust, my hair a matted, messy, mangled disaster. I never knew how good getting clean could feel.

After we were clean none of us wanted to get back into the filthy shifts the pirates had given us. I ordered them burned, then told the women to head for the Booty Hold and help themselves. I knew we had cases and crates of clothes. It was pretty funny, a couple dozen women running naked through the ship, trying hard to keep covered for modesty's sake. I couldn't care less who saw me unclothed right then, so I didn't bother trying to hide myself, chin held high, shoulders back. A couple of the younger girls saw me, saw how I was acting, and followed my lead. Some of the older women tsked, but no one said anything. We were too happy. Happy to be alive. Happy to be free.

We opened up the crates and cases and pretty much went wild. There were all kinds of things. Dresses, blouses, vest, coats. Underskirts, overskirts, bustles, petticoats, stockings, garters, bustiers. And corsets. Dozens of corsets in every colour, in every size and shape, in everything from silk to leather. One of the girls explained that their ship had been transporting an entire lingerie shops' merchandise as the shopkeep moved from Paris to Neptopolis, the capital of Atlan, the seat of government for the entire Empire.

I busied myself finding clothes. I found a cream cotton blouse and a black leather bustier to go over it. There was a bolero coat my size but for some reason no pants fit. Most were too long or else cut for men. I settled on a crimson satin skirt that I hiked up and tied in place with an extra set of garters. I pulled stockings over my legs and gartered them up too, then found a set of brown leather boots with white spats that fit perfectly.

Argenta didn't need clothes and Eve, for some reason, refused to part with her torn blouse and tattered skirt. Gigi managed to dig up a pair of cargo pants that she slit in the bum to allow her tail to slip through. A tank top and laced work boots completed her tough chick tomboy look. She even found an aviator cap that she cut holes into for her ears to poke out.

"Serena will need clothes too, miss," Eve reminded me.

"Yeah. She can have her pick when the sun goes down, I guess." Clean and dressed, I realized I was starving. "Let's get the ladies fed first, okay?"

"Yes, miss."

We went to the crew mess and feasted. There was all kinds of meats, cured, salted, jerkied, whatever would keep. Down in cold storage there was even some frozen meat, but no one wanted to wait for that to thaw, so we settled on a cold buffet of whatever we could find. Some of the women helped themselves to the wines and liqueurs we found. I had a celebratory glass of something red and sweet, then limited myself to watered down wine. Well, mostly water with a splash of wine in it. Call me paranoid, but I had an idea that the pirates who escaped might try to come back for their ship. Tyr Ebonfury in particular worried me.

But I couldn't deny the women their feast, either. I put Argenta in the wheelhouse, showed her how to steer the ship, told her to find a cloud bank and hide us there.

I went back to the mess, grabbed Gigi and pulled her aside. "How bad are the engines?"

She had a mouthful of greasy duck and gobbled it down before answering. "Bad? Why would they be bad?"

"You didn't damage them?"

"Damage them? No! I'd sooner destroy a work of art than damage this old beauty."

"The ship?"

"It's a real old workhorse. A lot of modifications, but it's basically an Anglic corsair. Eire make, of course. The best Anglic corsairs came out of Eire. She'll run as long as you keep her going."

"What'll it take to keep her going?"

"Stokers, mainly. Basic maintenance."

"Okay. Can I ask you to organize that? Once we've decided what we're doing with the pirates."

Her furry eyebrows knit together with worry, and she ducked her head. "I don't know that the women will follow me."

"Why not?"

"I'm an animan, remember?"

As if she wasn't covered in fur. With the face of a cat. "So?"

"So most humans don't like us."

"They followed you during the rebellion."

"Because I sounded like I knew what I was doing. And because you told them too."

"Right." I stood up and raised my voice. "How many of you speak Anglic?"

A few women raised their hands.

"Okay, so translate for me, please. My name is Sunset Val, in case you didn't already know. We've taken this ship. Now we need to run it. To run a ship, we need a crew, and we need a captain. Anyone know how to do that?"

Most of the women shook their heads. The others watched me, as if wondering where I was going with all this.

"Alright. I'm putting my name forward as captain. Anyone want to run against me?"

One of the women raised her hand.

"You want to be captain?" I asked.

"No!" she answered, eyes wide with sudden fright, shaking her head to make sure I understood. "I want to know why you want to race?"

"Race? What do you mean?"

"You asked if anyone wanted to 'run against' you."

Understanding dawned. "Oh! No, I meant, the captain should be voted for. Otherwise it's just another tyranny."

"Suffragist!" an older woman exclaimed. The women started murmuring.

I turned to Gigi and Eve, who'd come over to join us, still wearing her ragged clothes. "What's the big deal?"

"Women do not vote, miss."

"Why not?"

Gigi licked her hand and smoothed the grease out of her face. "It's not done."

"That's stupid." I turned to the others. "Look, I hate slavery. If that makes me an abolitionist, fine. I think women should vote. If that makes me a suffragist or whatever, also fine.

"You've had your lives taken away from you, by pistol and sword. Pirates wanted to make you slaves, sell you into a lifetime of servitude and pain. Your men, your brothers and husbands, fathers and sons, your sweethearts, they're gone. No one is going to make this decision for you. But we do have to decide."

It bothered me. They'd been trained since birth to believe that they couldn't think for themselves, couldn't vote, couldn't do anything but be good little wives and mothers. Women like Serena, who'd dedicated herself to mastering the sword, or Gigi, who'd gone to university to learn engineering, or even Diana and Dr. Enerva, who became pirates, all of them were considered freaks, aberrations of their society's natural order. It wasn't right. It wasn't fair.

They unanimously voted me in as captain. No one ran against me, which I didn't think was strictly speaking fair, but also considered kind of a compliment. I hoped.

"Okay. Any of you nurses? Midwives? Any sort of medical thing?" A couple of the girls raised their hands. "Eve, you take those two and sort out the surgeon's room. Get rid of the nastiness, okay? Clean it up. I'll send Argenta to help."

Eve looked down at me, big eyes filled with worry. "Oh no, miss, I can take care of it myself. No need to inconvenience anyone else."

I stepped closer to her and pitched my voice low so only she could hear. "Eve. I know you know what you're doing. But we need to get everyone working. Those two nurses will be your assistants once we make you ship's doctor, okay?"

Her whisper was more a hiss. "Ship's doctor? But miss, I'm not a doctor!"

"No, I know, but no one else knows half of what you do about anatomy, am I right? The way you patched up everyone after the fight, well, that tells me you're the one for the job."

She thought about it. "If you say so, miss. I mean, Captain."

I patted her shoulder. Her muscles were rock hard, the skin slightly clammy to the touch. "Thank you, Eve. I mean, Doc."

She smiled shyly and somewhat sadly, and I realized she must have been thinking of her creator. I smiled back, then turned to the others.

"You two go with the Doctor here. She'll show you what needs doing in the surgeon's room."

They nodded, obviously glad to have something useful to do, and just as glad to be told to do something. I realized then I'd have my work cut out for me, teaching these women to think for themselves.

Once Eve and her two nurses had gone, I said, "Okay ladies, here's the bad news. We still need stokers. I won't make anyone do it who doesn't want to. I know how nasty it is down there. But I also know this. Without stokers, the ship doesn't fly. So we're all going to have to work together. If you're not going to stoke, there are other, equally nasty jobs aboard a ship that will need doing. Hopefully Gigi can do something about the working conditions, but stoking is going to be hard, dirty, sweaty work."

"Why is *it* in charge?" one of the older women asked, looking at Gigi with obvious distaste. Beside me, I heard Gigi's low growl of displeasure.

"Does anyone else have an engineering degree?" I answered. No one did. "Gigi's studied engines. She knows how they work, and how to fix them. Can anyone else do that? No? That's why she's in charge. Now, who volunteers for the first shift?"

There was a long moment when I thought I'd have to assign them to stoke, but then a woman at the back raised her hand. Another joined her. Soon about a third of them had raised their hands.

"Thank you, ladies. Gigi, take them below and make sure the engines have a good head of steam in them. We're going to want to be able to outrun any pursuit."

Gigi nodded and grinned, then led the volunteers down to the engine room.

The rest I assigned basic chores, cooking and cleaning, that sort of thing, mostly to keep them out of my hair. I wanted to search the crew's quarters on my own. We hadn't gone into the captain's quarters yet. And I needed some time to think.

I relieved Argenta from the wheelhouse with a couple of the other girls, younger ones who seemed eager to prove themselves. They were about my age, I guessed. One of them said she'd worked on a ship before, as the first mate's yeoman. I didn't know what that meant, but it was good enough for me, so I put her on the wheel, with the other girl as backup.

Argenta, I set to guarding the slave quarters. Part of me wanted to go in there, to face the remaining pirates and rub it in their faces. The smarter part of me told that other part of me to stop being stupid and petty. I'm glad I listened to the smarter part.

I checked in on Serena. She was still completely unresponsive. I brushed a lock of pale hair out of her face, anxious for her to wake up. I missed her, even though it had only been a few hours. I was pretty exhausted, too. I guessed we all were.

I got some of the girls to clean up the main crew quarters, a big room with a half dozen bunk beds lining the walls. The pirates' personal stuff, we piled onto a dirty sheet, then two of the girls carried it all down into the

Booty Hold. We changed the sheets, opened the single porthole to let in some fresh air, then I told them to get some sleep. They followed the order gladly.

I went down to the engine room. The familiar pounding of the engine filled our auditory world. I found Gigi checking gauges and the women standing around, waiting with buckets full of coke. They'd all changed out of the feminine finery we'd found in the Booty Hold, or at least covered up with canvas overcoats.

As I watched from the door, Gigi turned and nodded to the women. She grinned and gave a thumbs up. The women grinned back and put down their buckets. Gigi went to each of them, taking their hand and patting their shoulder, saying something to them I was too far away to hear.

The women filed out, nodding to me as they passed. I nodded back. When they'd left I went to Gigi.

"You don't need stokers?"

She grinned, her cat face spreading wide in a human expression. "No, it's fine. Luke was an idiot. The engines were designed for minimal supervision. You want to see?"

I interrupted her before she could really get going. "Is there any chance someone who isn't trained in engineering will be able to understand and appreciate the finer points of what you're about to explain?"

Gigi thought about it, then shrugged. "Probably not."

"Okay. So let's just say, I appreciate what you've done and I think you're doing a great job. Thanks."

She looked surprised. "Oh! It wasn't all that much, actually. Give me a month to overhaul the ship completely and then I'll really surprise you."

"Well, we don't have a month. We need to figure out what to do with those pirates, first. Then we can figure out what to do about ourselves."

"What do you mean?"

I sat down on the stairs. Big mistake. Actually stopping for a rest made me very aware of how tired I was. Every muscle ached, and my head throbbed in time to the engines. Also, I was starving again. How did that happen? "These women have lives, you know? They're going to want to get back to them. Also, there's the very real chance that Tyr will come back and try to retake the ship. Our best bet would probably be to find an uninhabited coast somewhere, scuttle the ship and make our way inland. Try to find a city or something. Then the women can find their way home."

"Um."

"Um?"

"Well, I hate to be the one to break it to you, but there's really no going home, for any of us." She helped me to my feet and led me out of the engine room. Staring distastefully at the patch on her arm where the fur had been shaven off and a black crow tattoo stared back, she explained, "We've all got slave tattoos now. If we go into a city, we'll be stopped by the dock patrol and searched. As escaped slaves, we'll be sent into the gladiator pits." Her voice quieted, dimmed by some unnamed fear. "Women don't last long in the pits, whether human, animan, or anything else."

"God, is there anything nice in this world?"

"I saw a unicorn once! At the Albion Zoo."

"Wow, really?"

"He didn't look very happy, though. I think the city smoke was affecting his health."

I sighed, suddenly feeling very sorry for myself. It wasn't enough that I'd been stolen away from my own world, kidnapped by a mad scientist, captured by pirates, imprisoned, forced into slave labour, become a killer and led a rebellion. No, all this had to happen in a terrible world of tyranny, oppression, sexism, racism, and pollution that made unicorns sick. Great place.

I don't really do self-pity, though, so it didn't last long. Gigi led me up staircase after staircase until we stood outside a pair of wooden doors, bound with brass fittings and handled with the same brass crow motif as half the ship. I turned the handle.

The room past the doors was the captain's quarters, beautifully appointed with a huge four poster bed, white satin sheets, feather mattress and down pillows. Every finery stood carefully locked away in cabinets that lined the walls. Crystal goblets, gold plates, tiny bottles of precious scents captured in fine oils, exquisite porcelain sculptures, elegantly bound books in all shades of leather, all stood shoulder to shoulder and heaped in piles with no apparent order. Gems the size of the end of my thumb filled a soup bowl of cut crystal to overflowing. Necklaces were threaded through collections of rings and brooches. Jewelled daggers were stored with ivory handled pistols. Everywhere you looked, a fortune of luxury. It seemed that despite the austerity of his wardrobe, the unlamented late captain had been a bit of a magpie.

Gigi pushed me into the room with a playful grin. "Try and get some rest, Captain."

After I got over all the *Ooh Shiny!*, I went to the captain's desk. There were papers, letters, a huge ledger, a much smaller notebook, all of which were written in Atlan. I had to learn that language, and soon, or I'd go crazy.

I sat down on the bed to try and make sense of what the books said. A lot of it was numbers, and thank goodness those were the same. I thought one column was dates, and the next column was likely numbers of slaves taken or sold...

Chapter Twenty One

Making Decisions Is Hard Work

When I woke up, it was night.

"Velcome back."

Serena was sitting at the captain's desk, reading the papers I'd found by the light of a single, large electric light bulb. She'd found herself a pair of beige tights that fit like a second skin, a brilliantly white blouse worn under a crimson vest embroidered with hearts, and black leather boots that reached to her knees. Even sitting back with her feet crossed in front of her, one arm thrown casually over the back of the chair, she looked ready to pounce and kill.

"How long have I been asleep?"

"It is just past midnight. Since I do not know vhen you fell asleep, I cannot say how long it has been."

"Midnight?! Oh jeez, who's looking after the ship?"

"The crew are, Sunset Wal. Or should I call you Captain Wal?"

"Wal I mean, Val is fine, Serena." I sat up, somehow not very rested from my sleep. I could have just as easily curled back under the covers and slept until dawn.

"Wery vell, Wal. In private. In front of the crew, however, you must be Captain. Since that is vhat they have elected you."

"Yeah, because no one else wanted the job."

"Not true. Captain Crow certainly vanted the job. I have no doubt Tyr Ebonfury vanted it as vell."

"Well, one's dead and the other's probably coming after us."

"I think ve are safe for some time. It vill be veeks before he can recruit enough mercenary cutthroats to take back the ship. If he can find us."

"Yeah, I guess. But what do we do until then?"

"Just as you have been doing. Ve run. Ve hide."

"We still need to do something about the pirates we captured. Do we turn them in to the authorities?"

Serena made a face that expressed a lot of doubt as to the success of that idea. She picked up a folded letter. "There might be problems if ve do."

"What's that?"

"This? Is a letter of marque."

"Pretend for a second I don't know what that means."

She snorted out a laugh. "A letter of marque is official sanction to be a pirate. Someone in authority gave Captain Archibald Crow free reign of the skies."

"Someone in authority? Who?"

Serena glanced at the letter, then fixed me with a dry stare. "You vill not be surprised, I think. This letter is signed by the Minister of Ys himself, Maximillian Crow. The captain's brother."

"The captain who I killed. Great." I swung my legs off the bed and went to her, taking the letter she offered. Written in Atlan, of course, but the signature was legible enough. M. Crow, with words below that likely meant Minister of Ys. "Where's Yeeze?"

"Ys," she corrected me, rhyming it with Greece. "It is an island off the Gallian coast. A minor province with a reputation for lax legalities."

"So we can't go to the authorities. Or any place where there's likely to be people on the lookout for runaway slaves. Do you have any idea how to navigate?"

"None."

"Okay." I ticked things off on my fingers. "We need to find out where we are. We need to do something about those pirates. We need to know what the crew want to do, because if they all want to go home we can't exactly run the ship."

"Ve are escaped slaves, now. No matter that ve never had any owner beyond the slaver who took us."

"Yeah, that's what Gigi told me, too. Still, I'm willing to bet that there are some women who'd rather risk going home than live as fugitives. Besides, isn't there some way to get rid of the slave tattoo?"

"You could cut it off, but that vould leave an even more incriminating scar. And, you must remember. For most of these vomen, they have no home to return to. Their men are dead. To return home as an escaped slave vould shame their families."

"That's ridiculous! Why wouldn't their families be happy they're alive?"

"Human society is wery nuanced. I do not pretend to understand it."

"You were never human?"

"I am wampyri, you know this."

"No, I know. I just thought you got turned into a vampyri, is all."

"Wampyri are born like any creature. Except the animen. And patchworks."

"There, see? It wasn't so weird that I didn't know how you came to exist. Anyway." I blew a stray lock of hair out of my face. "In the morning we'll talk to the crew and find out what they want to do."

"You vill, you mean. I vill be taken by the slumber."

"Oh. Right." I chewed my bottom lip, thinking. "Serena, will you be my first mate?"

That surprised her. "I vould be honoured."

"I don't know how much of an honour it will be. You'll be in charge of the ship at night. At least, for as long as we have a crew. I need someone I can trust. I don't know any of the others. Eve, sure, and Gigi. But neither of them is especially cut out for command. And you, I've trusted since we met."

An unpleasant look flicked across her porcelain features, a look that said she had bad news and didn't really want to tell me. "There is a reason for this, Wal."

"Okaaaaaay."

"You gave your blood to me freely. This creates a bond between us."

"What? What kind of bond?"

"It is a psychic bond between the wampyri and the donor. It is a rare thing, for someone to villingly give their blood to a starving wampyri. You are lucky I did not kill you."

"Why didn't you tell me before?"

"I vould have told you but I vas half mad with the hunger."

"So, what, you can read my thoughts now?"

"No. It is more a general awareness. And it goes both vays. I know vhere you are, roughly. I know vhat you are feeling. Just as you know these things about me."

I realized she was telling the truth. There was a vague sense of worry coming from her, a fear that I would be angry, be terrified, exile her, or worse. Just as I realized that she was afraid of me and my reaction, my reaction of confusion that she thought I would ever feel that way about her calmed her fears. It was all very quick and a lot more complicated than I made it just sound, a kind of whirlwind of emotions and reactions.

"So, psychically bonded to a vampyri swordmistress. Could be worse."

"Do not joke, Wal. If I feed from you twice more, the bond, it is permanent and complete. You vill feel as I feel. You vill vish only to serve me, and feed me."

I nodded, all thoughts of joking quenched. "Okay, so, let's make sure that doesn't happen. Speaking of feeding, I'm starving. And also, how are we going to feed you?"

"I vill not need to feed for another veek or so. My kind have wery slow digestion."

"I, however, do not. I've got to eat something."

Serena casually waved at the dresser. "Von of the girls brought you some food vhile you slept."

A silver serving platter, the kind with the domed covers, sat on the dresser next to a bottle of wine and a crystal goblet. I went over and lifted the lid. Immediately the smell of something delicious assaulted my nose. Some kind of pie, the crust light and flaky, and inside, a rich brown gravy drowning chunks of some kind of tender meat and perfectly cooked vegetables. It had cooled enough that I wouldn't burn myself eating it. And I seriously ate it. I can honestly say I've never had a more delicious meal, and I scarfed it down in maybe five minutes. I soaked up the gravy with pieces of the most amazing bread I'd ever had in my life, just barely controlling myself from licking the dish clean.

I pulled open the wine and poured myself a half glass, looking for a pitcher to water it down. There was one on the night stand, specially designed to lock into place in a trio of circular grooves. It took me a little while to figure out how to get it out, and once I'd watered the wine I sensibly returned it to its place. I figured if a pitcher locked into place on an airship, there had to be a reason.

A vague sense of approval radiated from Serena, even though she busied herself with the papers on the desk. I got the impression it had something to do with my watered wine, but didn't ask her about it.

"So, the letters of marque. Are we in trouble? I mean, more trouble than runaway slaves normally are?"

"In trouble? Yes. But not vithout options."

"Like what?"

"There are places on the outskirts of the empire vhere ve can hide. Ve can keep to the skies, only wisiting ports that do not care vhether ve are escaped slaves or not. Ve can return to civilization, throw ourselves on the mercy of the courts, and hope." I didn't need the psychic bond between us to tell me all I needed to know about her opinion of our possibilities of success with that last option.

"So, where can we hide? Pirates have to know each other, right? Other slavers? They'll recognize the ship, think we're Captain Crow. At least, until Ebonfury gets the word out."

"True."

"So once the word is out, we're toast, right? The other pirates will gang up and come after us."

"Vhy vould they do that?"

Her question surprised me. I figured they would be pissed off that a bunch of rebellious slaves had gotten the better of one of their own, and told her so.

Her sneer said a lot about what she thought of the supposed honour amongst thieves. "Pah. I vould not vorry about it. They vould likely have a drink in Captain Crow's memory, then laugh at him for losing his ship to a bunch of vomen."

"So there's no fraternity of pirates? No special court that meets to settle pirate disputes and assign territories or whatever?"

"Vith a pirate king to rule them?" She laughed, high and light, a surprisingly girlish sound. "No Wal, it is not so civilized. Pirates settle disputes with cannon, gun, and sword. He who vins is windicated."

A thought that had been flitting around in my mind finally crystallized, fully formed. "Okay then."

"You've made a decision. I can feel it."

"Yeah."

"And this decision would be?"

I looked at her and grinned. "Let's become pirates."

Chapter Twenty Two

A Pirate's Life For Me

I outlined it for Serena. She liked it. We presented it to the crew just before dawn.

"So we pretend to be Captain Crow?" Gigi asked, repeating it in Atlan for the others.

"At first. Use his reputation for our own ends. Once word gets out he's attacking other slavers and pirates though, we'd have to do it on our own. Especially once word gets out that he's not us. Or we're not him. Whichever."

One of the women asked a question in Atlan, and Gigi translated. "How can we be pirates? None of us is trained on a ship or with a sword."

"Easy enough to train you for sword work. Serena's a swordmistress of the ninth order. I'm no slouch at the basic forms. Together we can whip you into shape in no time."

Some of them looked alarmed at my choice of words, so I explained that I didn't mean a literal whip.

Another woman asked, in heavily accented Anglic, "What if not want we being pirates?"

"You can return to your homes. We'll give you a share of the treasure we've got, and thank goodness for Mister Shorty's inventories, let me tell you. Once we've offloaded the Booty Hold, I'm told we can pretty much guarantee a comfortable life for ourselves, for a while. Or at least enough to get you home by train or another airship." That caused a lot of conversation.

It wouldn't be easy for them to get back home to wherever they were from. Maybe a third were Anglic, with a couple of Gallians and a bunch of Bavards. Three of the girls besides Serena and Eve had worked on ships before, including Molly, who hadn't said much since Dr. Enerva got away. Anglic, Gallia and Bavardy were a long way away from Merinasy.

See, Serena knew a place we could go, off the eastern coast of Afric, a place my memories of geography class told me was named Madagascar in my world and Merinasy here. There was a port town there, Libertia, that would rob us blind on the booty, but at least it would be gone. And we could trade for supplies and whatever else we needed. The women who wanted to leave could book passage on other ships, heading for Europa.

Luckily for us Libertia wasn't the only black market port in the world. Even more luckily, Captain Crow's maps had each port clearly marked. Once word got out that we were attacking other pirates, we'd need to keep on the move. Gigi assured me that wouldn't be a problem, so long as we weren't too damaged in any of the engagements. Our ship was good for years more service.

It was odd, being in a place where things were built to last instead of wearing out or getting obsolete in less than ten years. Back home, I'd been through three mp3 players, just since starting high school. My family had owned four different cars in the last ten years. Here, a ship stayed in service for decades, designed to stand the test of time, and lovingly cared for over the years. I can't tell you how many DVD players we threw away the second it stopped working right.

Anyway, we had other problems to deal with. Like the pirates still in our hold. Like half our crew wanted to go home. Honestly I was surprised it was only half. I'd want to go home, if I were them, but I couldn't. The only way home for me was somewhere at the bottom of the ocean, rusting away. So I was determined to make the best of my lot, which looked like becoming an airship pirate and sailing the seven skies.

I know what you're thinking. 'She's taking being torn away from her family and friends and the only life she's ever known really well.' Well, let me tell you, a lot of my time was taken up with thinking about what to do right then and there. It didn't leave a lot of room for thoughts of my Mom and Dad and sisters and stupid brother who was never on time picking me up anyway. There was even less room for thinking about my few friends. Also, I didn't have a lot of choice in the matter, right? I mean, how much moping around can one person do when they have absolutely no choices? Yeah, it really sucked, but I dealt with it, you know?

Okay, that's a lie. I bawled my eyes out later. But I'm getting ahead of the story, so let's get back to that.

Where was I? Oh right, the girls were talking about whether to stay or try and go home, living the lives of escaped slaves. After maybe fifteen minutes I asked for a show of hands, because time was moving on and

Serena's slumber would be taking her soon. I wanted the pirates off my ship before dawn. If they tried anything we'd have a swordmistress of the ninth order for them to deal with.

To my surprise, eventually only four women voted to try and go home. They were older, like older than my Mom, even, and not ready nor willing to embrace the aeronautical adventures of airship piracy.

That left us with less than two dozen women to run the entire ship. It should have worried me, but then, the pirates had done it with about the same number of crew and an untrained slave work force. Hopefully whatever slaves we liberated from other pirates and slavers, we'd get some recruits.

But first, the pirates had to meet with our justice.

Chapter Twenty Three

Walking the Metaphorical Plank

The debate over whether to strand them or kill them outright was long and heated. A lot of angry words, quite a few tears, some yelling, some crying. In the end, with dawn fast approaching and Serena already yawning, we voted to leave them on a deserted island.

It wasn't a mercy. I had no heart for cold-blooded murder, but if they died of starvation or dehydration, that didn't seem much better. My own opinion had wavered to and fro during the debate, one second for the mercy of murder, the next for marooning. It was a tight vote, with only two more votes for marooning.

"Look at it this vay," Serena said with another alarming yawn. The slumber would be on her too soon. "Perhaps they vill turn to cannibalism and survive."

"That's disgusting."

"It happens all the time, though," Gigi added unhelpfully. "At least, among humans and animen. I can't say much for patchworks or vampyri, and of course automatons don't eat."

"Can we change the subject please?"

I nodded to Eve and she spun open the lock on the door. I had my pistol out, ready to blast away at anything that moved. Serena had a sword in each hand, looking totally bad-ass even if she was about to pass out. Just a few more minutes and we'd be rid of these pirates.

Turned out Molly had some knowledge of how to navigate by maps and instruments. Her father had been a ship's captain before something called the blight took him when she was young. No one would explain to me what the blight was. I guessed it was some kind of sickness. For all their advanced technology on this world, they didn't seem to have any shortage of weird physical ailments and other issues. Probably due to doctors removing legs to repair gashed shins. Sort of a baby with the bathwater decision, I thought.

Anyway, Molly managed to figure out where we were, and it turned out we weren't far from a whole string of uninhabited islands. There were a lot more islands on this world than I remembered there being in the Atlantic Ocean, but then, North America was shattered in two and what I thought of as New England was a lot closer to Actual England, that is, Anglic, than it was back home.

So we lowered ourselves down until we were flying along about a hundred feet above the rough seas below. Down near the ground, the wind was a lot worse, and I had to order Argenta to take the wheel and hold us steady. We left a couple of girls there to help direct her. Argenta would do anything she was told but she didn't have a whole lot of initiative. I wanted to leave Molly with her as navigator, but she wouldn't even hear me out, insisting she be allowed to witness the pirates' final justice.

Gigi and her stokers were working the engines hard. Which left Serena, a gang of girls looking for some payback, and myself to bring the pirates from the former slave quarters to drop them out the launch bay.

Eve opened the door and we braced for some kind of attack, but we needn't have bothered. The pirates were sitting on the floor. Some of them lay on the mats, asleep. Diana noticed us first, raising her head from where she was resting it against her knees. She saw my pistol and Serena's swords and I swear, she started to cry.

The big bad pirate bitch, crying. God, she had to go and make it harder than it already was.

"Up!" Serena ordered, her voice echoing in the mostly empty room. The pirates got to their feet, kicking their companions awake.

My crew got in among them, tying their hands behind their backs. Dreads didn't offer any resistance. Diana had to be dragged to her feet, silent tears streaming down her face.

We marched them to the launch bay. I ordered the bay doors opened, then sent one of the girls to tell Argenta to lower the ship.

The seas were rushing past us, below. I smelled the salt air, felt the spray as waves crashed together beneath us. The ship rocked and shook, buffeted by the winds that howled across the open bay doors. My hair whipped at my face, dancing in the wind. I grabbed a set of goggles and pulled them on to keep from being blinded. I'd have to find something to keep my hair under control.

Suddenly there was a beach about twenty feet below us. Serena looked at me. I stared at the pirates. Part of me wanted to condemn them officially. Part of me wanted to vomit at what I was about to do. In the end, I couldn't speak, so I just nodded.

Serena turned and grabbed the first pirate. She shoved him toward the waiting bay. He walked slowly. A couple of times she had to jab him with the point of her sword. There wasn't any plank for him to walk, like they had in the movies, but we were making him walk the plank just the same.

At the last second Serena slit the ropes binding his hands, then gave him one last shove. He leapt out the open bay doors. We hurtled past him before he landed, so I had no idea if he had a hard or soft landing. I discovered I didn't care.

The tiny nugget of anger deep inside me suddenly erupted into red-hot rage. How dare they? How dare they make me feel pity for them? How many lives had they destroyed? Not just the countless slaves they'd stolen and sold, but all those slaves' families, wondering whatever had become of their womenfolk? And all the men they'd killed on all the ships they'd taken, men who had been too much trouble to allow to live?

I hardened my heart as the rest were made to jump. Some went quickly, their need to have the waiting over with outweighing their fear of dying from the fall. Some went reluctantly, every step like lead bricks were tied to their feet. Some fought, like Dreads, and had to be subdued and dragged to the bay doors before being tossed out unceremoniously.

As for Diana, she surprised me. She shook off her guards and ran for me. Serena was by my side in a heartbeat, sword raised, but Diana fell to her knees.

"Please," she begged, voice raised over the sound of the howling winds.

"You expect me to let you stay on the ship?"

"No, no, not that. There is a pictoriogram in my quarters. Of me and my sister. Please let me take it with me. Please, I'm begging you. She's the only family I have. Let me die with her image to ease the passage."

I thought the anger that burned in my heart couldn't get any hotter. I was right, it didn't get any hotter. It got cold, a burning white cold in my heart, searing my soul.

I leaned in close so she would be sure to hear me, raised my goggles to stare her in the eyes. "How many women did you tear away from their sisters?"

The blood drained out of her face. She tilted her head back and closed her eyes. Tears spilled down her face. I glanced at the two girls standing to either side of Diana, then with a twitch of my head I ordered them to throw her out. They had to drag her. She wouldn't stand, but went limp when their hands grabbed her arms, a dead weight. All the arrogance, all the fight had drained out of her. I've never seen anyone so completely defeated. I found myself hoping the fall would kill her, the only sliver of mercy I felt.

My girls tossed her through the bay doors without any ceremony or hesitation. Diana was the last. I ordered the doors closed.

"Serena, go get some sleep." I picked a girl at random. I would really need to learn everyone's names. And Atlan. "You speak Anglic? Okay, tell the pilot to set a course due south. Take us at least a hundred miles from this place, then turn east. I'll be in my quarters."

I held it together all the way to my quarters on the topmost deck. Once I'd closed the doors behind me, the tears came. I tossed myself on the huge bed and wept.

Chapter Twenty Four

Lunch Break

After a morning of crying and feeling sorry for myself and a short nap, I washed my face in the bowl of water set on my dresser. I felt better than I had in days. Guess I needed to let it out. Of course, letting it out seemed to have made room for me to be starving, again, so I made my way down to the crew mess hall to see if I couldn't find something to eat.

What I found amazed me. A couple of the women, a mother and daughter from their similar features and differing ages, had taken it on themselves to become our ship's cooks, and they set out a spread like I'd never seen. Pies dripped rich brown sauce. Roast chickens lined up, ready to be eaten. Bowls filled with every vegetable you can imagine, chopped up and smothered in some kind of sticky sweet sauce. Fresh bread baked just that morning, still hot enough to melt butter.

Neither of the cooks spoke any Anglic. I got their names from them, at least, Brunhilde and her daughter Hilda, both built on the big, blonde, and blue eyed model. I thanked them profusely as I filled my plate and dug in. Hilda went and pushed a button set near the door. A buzzer went off, and a few seconds later a gang of women arrived, ready to eat.

I must have slept longer than I thought, because this was the midday meal. The women helped themselves to the feast and sat down, chatting amicably. Eve was one of them. There wasn't enough room at the table for everyone, so she sat awkwardly on a low wooden chair in the corner, her long legs bending too steeply to allow her lap to serve as a table.

I finished my first plate and got up for seconds. It was all so delicious I don't think I would have been able to resist, even if I hadn't been starving. My plate refilled, I went and stood near Eve, who tried to stand and offer me her seat. Sitting, even on the low chair, she was nearly as tall as I was standing.

I put a hand on her shoulder to keep her sitting. "Sit down, I'm perfectly fine."

"You're injured, Captain, you should be resting."

"There are girls aboard more injured than me, Eve. I can stand, and you've earned yourself a rest."

"If you insist, Captain."

"I do."

As we ate I asked about the state of our injured crew. Most had simple cuts and gashes. One had broken her wrist. One had been stabbed in the back and had fluid in her lung. Eve wasn't very optimistic about that one. And of course, Molly had lost an arm, a leg, and an eye.

"The workmanship of her prosthetics is flawless, absolutely flawless," Eve said, wiping her mouth with a napkin. "The highest craftsmanship. Anatolyne make, or Levantian, I'm sure of it. I'd ask Gigi, but she's quite busy with the engines. Her eyelens is nothing like any I've ever seen. It may well have come from Zhou, or even Neppon. And say what you will of her, but Dr. Enerva was a brilliant physician. The implantations show no sign of further festering or rejection."

"So Molly's alright?"

"Physically she is as healthy as can be, Captain."

"How about psychologically?"

Eve looked away, busying herself with juggling her napkin, her plate, and her mug of tea all at once. She managed well enough, taking a sip of the fragrant tea, then looked up at me. "I'm really not qualified to judge her mental state, Captain."

"Is she still muttering about killing Enerva?"

She looked away again, but nodded.

"Okay. Well, keep an eye on her. Revenge isn't the best reason to stay alive, but it's a reason. We'll just have to give her more reasons."

I gave her shoulder a squeeze and she seemed startled by the gesture of familiarity. Startled, but pleased.

I saw that the women were mostly finished eating so I gave the order to switch shifts and relieve their companions still at their posts. They followed my order quickly and efficiently, cleaning up after themselves and even resetting the table. I was still getting used to giving orders, and they were already a crew.

Yeah, it was pretty awesome. There I was, seventeen years old, already captain of my own airship. How cool was that? Of course, there was the whole people trying to kill me thing, but you've got to take the bad with the good, am I right?

On my way out of the mess hall, pausing only to thank Brunhilde and Hilda again for their incredible meal, I felt the ship start to turn. The hard left I'd ordered, I hoped, as I hurried toward the wheelhouse.

We were turning hard left, but not because of my order. When I entered the wheelhouse, one of the girls said in accented Anglic, "Ship to starboard, Captain."

"Thanks, um?"

"Viola, Captain."

I turned to the other girl, who like Viola had long dark hair. "And you?"

"She does not speak Anglic, Captain," Viola explained. "But she is named Domina."

And people kept saying I had a weird name. Anyway.

"Who told Argenta to turn?"

"Me, Captain," came a quiet voice from the corner. It was Molly, sitting behind some kind of control panel. When we'd gotten our new clothes, she'd chosen a lot of black and red. She had combed her long brown hair over so that it hung over her eyelens, hiding both it and the scar on the side of her head. Her prosthetics were hidden under her heavy red brocade coat, loose black skirt and black leather thigh boots.

"Molly," I greeted her with a nod and a smile of approval. It didn't do anything to remove the scowl she wore.

She stood with the help of a crutch, lips pressed together in suppressed pain. Favouring her prosthetic, she limped over to where I stood by Argenta, staring all the while out the starboard windows at what I first thought was nothing. I squinted and saw what she was looking at, a dark speck in the blue sky. Below, the ocean glittered.

"Anyone got any binoculars?" I asked.

Viola handed me a set of goggles with intricate lens set in brass holdings.

I took them from her. "Oh hey, cool. Thanks."

I slipped the goggles over my head and adjusted the lenses. It took me a couple of seconds to find the neighbouring ship again. It was a lot like ours, built like a sailing ship without a mast or sails, slung under a huge sausage-like balloon, driven by a giant propeller at the rear. Their figurehead was a mermaid, with blue writing painted near the mermaid's shoulder. It must have been the ship's name, but even with the goggles it was too small, too far away, to make out. It made me wonder.

"Hey, what's the name of our ship, anyway?"

"The Captain Crow, he name it The Carrion," Viola answered.

"Wow, that's a terrible name for a ship. Okay, tonight we'll vote on a new name. They've got a mermaid for a figurehead. Sound familiar to anyone?" No one answered. A sudden series of flashes of light burst from the ship. "Hey, they're flashing us. Anyone speak flashy?" I pushed the goggles onto my forehead. "No?"

Viola and Domina shook their heads. Molly ignored me, just staring at the ship.

"Molly?"

She jumped, startled, and turned to me. "Apologies, Captain. I thinking."

"I could see that. About what?"

"That ship. What if they be," she paused, then said grimly, "Pirates?"

"Slavers, too, maybe," Viola added.

"Viola, ask Domina to go get Gigi. She's probably in the mess."

"Aye Captain," she answered, turning to the other girl and speaking in rapid Atlan.

As Domina left the wheelhouse, I slipped one goggle lens over my right eye and looked for the ship again. "They've turned toward us."

Molly swore something so vile in Atlan that Viola paled, shocked. I wished Serena were here. She'd know what to do.

But I was the captain. I had to make the decision.

"Viola, ring the engine room. Full steam ahead."

Chapter Twenty Five

Running Away

Viola cranked the dial thing that called down to the engine room, ordering full steam.

"What you mean do, Captain?" Molly asked.

"Find out if Gigi speaks flashy. Maybe she can tell us what they want. Maybe not. Either way, we're running for it."

Molly was looking out the window again. "What if they be slavers?"

"We're in no condition for combat, Molly. Half the crew is still sleeping off yesterday's battles. Half are eating lunch. There's still blood on our decks. A lot of us are injured. And don't forget, none of us really knows how to fight. We got lucky yesterday, because they weren't expecting us to rebel, couldn't believe that a bunch of women would have the nerve to do anything more than meekly accept our fate."

"We could trap. Let board, and corner."

"If they're slavers they wouldn't want us, anyway. We're already tattooed, remember? The second they found out they'd slaughter us all as more trouble than we're worth, then sell our parts to the nearest patchwork factory.

"If they're just pirates, they'd want the ship and slaughter us for the booty in our hold. The sooner we get rid of that the happier I'll be, let me tell you. No, we run. As hard and fast as we can."

"Run away." Molly's face was fierce with frustration and fury. She slammed her mechanical fist against the wall with the clash of metal on metal. "AWAY?!"

I could have sworn she dented the wall. I glared at her, ice in my eyes. "That's enough."

Gigi stepped through the open door, carrying a plate of roast chicken. "You asked for me, Captain?"

"Oh, right, you're not in the engine room." Molly limped past me and out the door. She was going to be trouble, I knew it. "Can you read the flashy talk ships use?"

"Um, no?"

"Okay. Get below and give me full steam. We're running from that ship over there."

"Where?"

I pointed out the window. She squinted. I passed her the goggles. She held them to her eyes with one hand, rather than try to put them on.

"Nice ship. Not Eire made, but nice enough. Probably Hispanian. They're supposed to prefer female figureheads."

"What's ours, anyway?"

"You haven't seen it? Not even when you were taken?"

"No, it was night, and during a storm."

"The Carrion's got a blighted crow, of course. Festering and fearful, like our former captain."

"Nice. Well, our mermaid friends can suck our tail-feathers. Get us out of here, Gigi."

"Aye, Captain."

She left, still carrying the roast chicken. I turned to Viola and Domina. "You two go get fed. Send two girls who can speak Anglic well enough to start teaching me Atlan."

Viola translated for the other girl, then turned to me. "Aye Captain."

They left me alone with Argenta. I went over to her. "Argenta, do you need a rest?"

Her thinking engine, processor, whatever it was called here, whirred and clicked and eventually she shook her head.

As I stood there, waiting for the engines to really start pounding, I thought about what we were doing, going over the decision in my mind. No, it was the right choice to make. We were in no condition to take on a potential threat. Not that I had any proof they were a threat, of course.

I checked the skies for the other ship. They were definitely gaining on us, rising in altitude to our level.

"Come on, Gigi."

A couple of women stepped into the wheelhouse, an older woman with greying hair tied back in a tight bun and a girl about my age with dark hair and dark skin. They both had an amused twinkle in their eyes and smiles on their lips, like this was all a grand adventure.

"I am Miss Mattis Merryweather, Captain," the older woman introduced herself with a small curtsy.

"Pleased to meet you. And you?"

"Salia Nazir, my Captain," she answered, nodding her head toward me. Her accent was different from everyone else's I'd heard so far.

"Okay Salia, take these goggles and keep an eye on that ship." I handed her the goggles and pointed out the ship. "If they so much as blink at us, I want to know about it."

"As you command, my Captain."

"Your Anglic is excellent."

"I have an excellent instructor, my Captain."

"Thank you, child."

I turned to Miss Merryweather. Something about her kept me from even thinking of her as Mattis. "You're an instructor?"

"Among many things, Captain, I am."

"Including an Atlan instructor?"

She said something in Atlan.

I stared at her blankly. "I think it's best to assume I've never had any Atlan instruction whatsoever."

"Ah," she answered. "Well then, let us begin at the beginning."

But before she could start my lessons, the dial next to the wheel that indicated how fast we were going rang like a bicycle bell and clicked from 'Cruising' to 'Half Power'.

"Argenta, take us up, into the clouds."

Argenta nodded and twisted at the waist without moving her feet, then cranked a handled wheel until the dial next to it proclaimed an upward angle of fifteen degrees. I didn't feel any change in the angle of the deck, but then, I didn't really understand how the ship worked, either.

"Okay, Miss Merryweather, let's do this."

What followed was a distracted lesson on Atlan, mostly in Atlan. Repetition seemed to be the key to learning in this world, and all we did was repeat verbs over and over. I am, you are, he is, she is, we are, they are, sort of thing, over and over again until my head was spinning. All the while trying to outrun a presumed pirate.

After a couple of dizzying hours, I'd gotten the gist of how Atlan worked with changing the verbs, so naturally that's when Miss Merryweather started introducing the irregular verbs, the ones that didn't follow the same rules. And we hadn't even started on verb tenses. Great.

Gigi had sent up word that she needed stokers, so I'd sent Salia out to round up volunteers. She came back saying that volunteers hadn't been hard to find, since a lot of the women didn't quite know what to do with themselves. I sent down orders to clean out the ship, starting with our former captors' quarters. Everything down to the Booty Hold. We'd sell it all off and split the money. After that, they should start scrubbing down the bloodstains that seemed to be everywhere. Then I asked Miss Merryweather for a break and went down to the crew quarters myself.

It wasn't hard to find Diana's quarters. I found the whatever she'd called it, the pictoriogram, which was basically an old style sepia photograph in an ornate oval frame. She'd kept it in her footlocker. It showed Diana and her twin sister, younger and happier. As the quarters began to fill with cleaners eager for something to do, I snagged one of the girls and told her to carry the photo to my quarters. Also I told her to leave my quarters for last, and to spread the word. Then I went back to the wheelhouse.

The window was blank white. I could have sworn a chill crept through me. My imagination of course, since the temperature in the wheelhouse hadn't really changed, but flying through the clouds reminded me of a big dead bully impaled on a boat hook. I managed with difficulty to keep from shivering, and asked Miss Merryweather to continue with her lessons.

We lost them, sometime before supper.

I nodded, mostly to myself. "Due east, Argenta."

Chapter Twenty Six

So You Think You Can Dance?

Once we'd made the full turn due east, I ordered we return to cruising speed, then left the wheelhouse. I went to my quarters, my brain whirling with verb conjugations and noun genders. At least I spoke a little French, so I understood the use of gender to designate nouns.

About a half dozen women were in my quarters, cramming Captain Crow's collection into sacks to carry down to the Booty Hold. I gave them a hand, happy to see the last remnants of my predecessor gone. All I kept were the books and maps, and a couple of pairs of goggles, including one with darkened lenses to shield against the glare of the sun. Everything else went, leaving behind a remarkably empty and surprisingly calm cabin.

While I was down in the Booty Hold, I noticed one of the women taking a careful inventory. She was small and stout, and I instinctively nicknamed her Mrs. Shorty, though I would never use it to her face. Her name was Elegiac Throckwaddle, and she'd been a merchant's wife before she'd been taken a slave.

"Okay then, Mrs. Throckwaddle, I'll leave our inventory in your capable hands." Then I tried some Atlan, trying to tell her she'd done a good job. From the look on her face and the giggles I heard behind me, my Atlan needed some improvement.

I left everyone who'd helped me in the Booty Hold to help Mrs. Throckwaddle and I returned to my cabin. I looked at the charts and maps, hoping they would suddenly make sense. We'd be crossing Afric soon, and I needed to know where to go and how to avoid other ships. I needed to know how to get all the way across an entire continent undetected, how to arrive at Libertia without being found and killed by other pirates. And when Captain Crow's brother found out what we'd done, I would bet the entire contents of the Booty Hold he'd come after us. Because even though my stupid brother was so stupid, he was my brother. If someone killed him (besides me, that is, if I ever got back home), I'd hunt them down and kill them back twice as hard.

Afric was a huge continent of deserts and jungles, of plains and mountains. Pretty much like Africa back home, only this continent hadn't been invaded by Europeans and criss-crossed with railroad lines. Afric had a thousand tiny tribal kingdoms, all united under the banner of the Atlan empire. Just like pretty much half the planet.

According to the maps I found, Atlan controlled most of Europa, except for the Norsic kingdoms way up north; half of Russankya; all of Afric, including the Saud, Levantia, and Anatolyne; the Raj of Hindyastan; the southern half of Zhou; and of course all of itself, basically the entire eastern seaboard of what back home would have been the United States and Canada. And right there, north of Atlan, west of Gallia, about the same size as Eire, was Ys, firmly under the Empire's thumb. I'm not afraid to say it impressed me. Too bad we had to avoid civilized places because they would check for runaway slaves. Too bad the supposedly civilized places even used slaves.

I studied the map of the Sahar Desert, not really looking forward to trying to cross it. It wasn't nearly as huge as back home, but it still pretty much covered the entire length of Northern Afric, from the Atlan Sea across to Aegyptia. A couple of watering holes were indicated on the map, and a couple of trading camps, if I read it correctly. But other than that, the desert was a big empty nothing of heat and sand. And potentially, death.

I really needed to talk to Serena. She'd spent time on a ship. At least, as an active member of the crew and not just a cleaning woman or cook's assistant. Molly was a captain's daughter, and knew how to navigate a little, but she was kind of psycho, and all she wanted was revenge. And maybe to die. I still wasn't sure about that.

It occurred to me that having a first mate who was asleep half the day was less than ideal, but I didn't really know who else I could trust to do the job.

Libertia suddenly seemed like a bad idea. It was too far, would take too long to get there. We needed to get rid of our booty as soon as possible. We needed to offload the women who wanted to get home just as quickly. If we encountered another ship and couldn't outrun them, we were toast. We'd gotten lucky with our captors. We wouldn't be so lucky again.

The dinner bell rang. I went down to the crew mess. Brunhilde and Hilda had outdone themselves, cooking up a feast fit for royalty. And desserts! Cakes and pies and some kind of strudel things. I made sure everyone had a chance to eat their fill, then asked Miss Merryweather to translate my profuse thanks and admiration to the mother and her daughter. Both beamed with pride. Brunhilde explained through Miss Merryweather that normally she wouldn't make so much food, but our stores were on the verge of going bad. Soon we'd be back to heavily salted stews and soups and sauces, but while we had the fruits and vegetables, we'd eat them up. If she could get some more supplies she'd be jamming and pickling as much as she could. I told her we'd look into it once we'd sold off our booty.

"Alright girls, once the sun's set, we start sword training. We can't defend ourselves and we can't attack any slavers out there without some kind of training. Anyone interested should report to the former slave quarters an hour after sundown."

As it turned out, the sun had just about set, so I headed down to Serena's quarters. She'd managed to clean out the former occupant's belongings, leaving just a bunk and a footlocker. She'd left me the only key into her quarters, a sign of her complete trust in me. Vampyri paranoia is what keeps them safe from ignorant peasants, she'd explained.

I unlocked the door just as she sat up. She jumped to her feet, snarling, but relaxed when she saw it was me.

"Ah, Captain. Good evening."

"Hi Serena. Want me to give you a few minutes to get dressed?"

"If you vould be so kind."

It didn't take nearly that long. I had just closed the door and turned around to lean against the wall when it opened again, revealing a washed and dressed Serena.

"Wow. That was quick."

"Yes. How can I be of assistance, Captain?"

"Want to take a walk in the night air?"

"As you vish."

We went up on deck. The night air was frigid and the wind was bitter, but I'd snagged a set of goggles to keep my hair out of my eyes. I could have used one of the aviator caps we had, but my increasingly tangled mane of red hair wouldn't fit under it.

Serena, of course, barely noticed the chill, and with a deft motion bunned up her long pale hair. She nearly glowed in the moonlight, silver light reflecting off her pale skin and hair.

Far below us, a silver desert stretched out for miles and miles. Dunes scarred the landscape with black shadows. Both incredibly beautiful and indescribably depressing, the desert disappeared into darkness in every direction. I leaned against the railing and sighed.

"Do not vorry, Wal." Serena rested a cautious hand on my shoulder, as though unaccustomed to the familiarity of a comforting touch.

"Worry about what? The pirates chasing us, our untrained crew, potential governmental retribution? Diminishing food supplies? The continent that lies between us and theoretical safety?"

"Pirates are always chasing airships. The crew begins its training tonight. Minister Crow vill seek his revenge as he sees fit. Food supplies are always diminishing. And there is no such thing as safety. There. Feel better?"

I looked at her, unsure if she was joking or not. She had an incredible poker face, but after a long moment of incredulous silence, her full lips quirked into a barely suppressed grin. I laughed, and she joined me.

"You should know. During my slumber, I vas aware of you. Your decisions, your emotions. Like a dream, they came to me. You made the right decision to avoid that ship. I understand some luminosignalization, not much, but some. Next time, write down the signals in terms of how many short and long flashes of light you see. I vill attempt to translate vhen I have awoken."

"I was thinking about that. What if," I bit my lower lip, unsure how to put my thoughts and emotions and half formed plans into words.

"Vhat if ve vere to switch from a day shift to a night shift? That is vhat you vanted to say?"

I grinned at her. "Yeah, I guess it is. Hey, that's pretty useful."

"Yes, I imagine it vill be of some use, Walerie."

I froze. I hadn't told anyone in this world my real name.

"You need not fear me, Walerie. Your thoughts vhen I am awake are harder to hear. During my slumber, though, there is less, you vould say, interference. Your secret is safe. Your vorld is strange and confusing to me, and I do not understand how you got here. But your being from another vorld does explain many things. Your inability to speak Atlan, and your ignorance of even the most basic facts of our vorld. Also your radical ideas about the place for vomen and nonhumans in society, and for the eradication of slavery. Vorthy goals, yes? None of the former slaves aboard this ship could have done vhat you have done."

I took a deep breath. "Thanks."

She grinned, and I saw fangs this time. "Besides, the blood link between us makes getting caught up all the easier, no? I already know vhat you have to tell me. Molly vill be fine, in time. She is angry, it is understandable. The vomen vill learn vhat ve need them to learn. First, the sword, yes?"

"Yeah. What do you think of our becoming a nocturnal ship?"

"It vill certainly make my being involved in any action all the easier."

"Yeah, okay. Cool."

"It certainly is, judging by your temperature."

"My temperature?"

"Wampyri can see the heat of living bodies, and yours is diminishing."

"Okay then, let's get inside."

At supper, I'd ordered the girls who were keenest on weapons training to clean out our former slave quarters. I led Serena down there, by way of the weapons locker. As I pulled the key out of my jacket pocket, Serena stopped me.

"No need. Tonight is not for swords. Tonight is for dancing."

"Dancing?"

"How else vill ve see who vill pad like a cat and who vill plod like a cow?"

"Okay, you're the boss. In weapons training, that is."

Down in the new training room, the girls had outdone themselves. Gone were the mats we'd slept on, scrubbed away the stench of sweat and tears and worse. An empty room, filled with hopeful and eager faces.

Not everyone was so keen. Several of the older women seemed remarkably reluctant to even be there, edging to the sidelines and wallflowering there with crossed arms and disapproving looks.

Serena asked after the contents of Dr. Enerva's cabin, then left us there to follow Mrs. Shorty into the Booty Hold. They came back a couple of minutes later, carrying a couple of large wooden boxes. One opened up to reveal a phonograph, an old fashioned kind of record player. Instead of playing flat disks, there were several long black cylinders stored in the other box. Serena loaded one onto the phonograph and turned the crank. Scratchy classical music began to play.

One by one, Serena danced with each of us. Some of the women knew how to dance, and some of them could dance really well. Others, like me, seemed to be born with two left feet. Of course, it didn't help that I'd never learned how to fancy dance. I'd been to a couple of school dances, that's all, and let me tell you, grinding up against a guy you like isn't anything like waltzing around with a vampyri.

The only people not present were Argenta and Molly, who I'd left in the wheelhouse, and the patients left in the surgeon's quarters. Everyone else had a turn, no matter their age or background or genetic make-up. Which meant, even Gigi. To no one's surprise, the cat animan was pretty nimble on her feet.

Eve, however, surprised everyone. At first she just clunked around in her big thick soled boots, barely keeping up with Serena. After a few steps, she asked for a break, pulled off her boots, and returned to the dance. Unburdened by the weight of her boots, she spun and twirled around the dance floor, taking Serena's lead like she'd been born to dance. I even caught her closing her eyes and grinning so beautifully it erased the ugliness of her scars and stitches. Everyone applauded when they stopped dancing. Eve did that shy smile, tucked chin thing she did whenever she was embarrassed.

By the end of the evening, Serena had divided us into two groups. She determined that about a dozen of us, myself included, were agile enough not to kill ourselves with a real sword. The rest would need basic training in the beginner forms, something I could teach during the day.

It was getting pretty late. Close to midnight, in fact. I noticed a couple of the older women stifling yawns. I called for an end to our training.

"Good job, girls, good job." I led them in a round of applause for themselves, something they seemed surprised and delighted by. Self-appreciation was something else I wanted to teach them.

I picked out two of the girls around my age and put them on night watch with Serena, with orders to wake me if anything happened. Then I went back to my quarters, washed myself in the bowl on the night stand, climbed into bed and fell fast asleep.

Chapter Twenty Seven

Heading Toward a Feast of Flesh

We changed course. For three days, we flew due south, cleaning up during the day, practising with sticks instead of swords and dancing at night. Gradually we shifted our waking hours so that we'd basically sleep away the morning to be able to stay up later at night. I told the crew that we'd be shifting to a full-on night crew eventually, and they seemed to take it without fuss, though a couple of the older women volunteered for permanent day shift.

When I say the older women, I mean, the oldest was Miss Merryweather, and she couldn't have been a day older than forty five. Her hair was grey and her face and hands were pretty wrinkled, but otherwise she carried herself with none of that excessive care of the elderly. She'd been one of the ones who'd made it into the first dozen sword trainees, put it that way.

Serena and Molly had a few long talks during the nights that followed that first dancing lesson, and Molly seemed to calm down a little. She and Serena had special training sessions to help Molly learn to use her prosthetics to her advantage in a fight, which channelled a lot of Molly's rage and hate into something productive.

During the day, the oppressive heat of the dry desert air drove us below, which wasn't much better. Opening all the windows didn't help, either. Gigi warned me that the engines were dangerously close to overheating, so I ordered them slowed to a crawl during the day, hoping the wind wouldn't blow us too much off course. At night, we stoked the fires and got us up to full speed, gaining what ground we'd lost during the day.

And then, with a surprising suddenness, the desert disappeared behind us, changing abruptly from sandy dunes to scrub grasslands, and then just as quickly to the lush greenery of the tropical jungle canopy. Ahead lay mountains, purple-grey against the heat hazed white sky.

"Here," Serena said on our fourth night overland, pointing at a spot on a map. It looked like mountains to me. She and I had escaped the heat of my quarters by heading into the wheelhouse with the maps. Somehow the day's heat never disappeared with the oncoming night. At least, not inside the ship.

"Mountains."

"At the base of these mountains is a city known to flaunt the laws of Atlan. A willainous place of cutthroats and thieves. Everything is for sale there, and life the cheapest of all."

"What's the name of this place, and why are we going there? And how will you find it?"

"Hearsay evidence, sailors' tales, and hopefully a little luck." Serena stared at the map, as though willing it to show the city she spoke of. "Vhere the jungle grows from the desert, at the base of the mountains, three days from the river of rivers, vhere the lion and lamb meet to feast on the flesh of the dead."

"Djen," Molly said, leaning forward on her crutch. She favoured the wheelhouse as her hangout. "You talk Djen."

"Yes.

I'd never heard of it. Big surprise. "Okay, what's all that about feasting flesh?"

"This," Serena pointed. More mountains. "This mountain is known as the Lamb's Head. And this, these plains. Lions dwell there, in abundance."

"Get to the flesh feast, please?"

"If I remember my history correctly, once a great Atlan legion marched across these plains, seeking Djen. Thirst killed many, and many more died of disease, before the varriors of Djen destroyed the rest. Lions are not fussy about who kills their food."

"Yeah, okay, but that river there? It's not that far."

"Not by airship, no. By foot? Perhaps three days."

"Okay, so, Djen it is."

"Djen bad place," Molly argued. "Very bad. Much go wrong."

"There vill be caravaneers on their way to Tombutu, taking land routes back to the shipping ports. The vomen who vish to leave may do so. Ve vill be rid of the treasures in our hold, ve can buy supplies. Then, ve take to the air and hunt. The predators become the prey, yes?"

"Much very bad," Molly said, but there was a glimmer of eagerness in her natural eye at the thought of preying on the predators of the air.

At any rate, my mind was made up. "Set a course, Molly. We're going to Djen."

Chapter Twenty Eight

Trading for Lives

Djen turned out to be not far from where Serena had estimated it would be, though it was harder to find than that. Pretty much because the plains ended miles from where it said they ended on the map. Jungle had grown at the foot of the mountains, and the entire town of mud brick huts was under the tree canopy. Not that easy to spot from the air. The only thing that gave it away was the thin white smoke rising from their cook pots, and a couple of ornies flitting around. As we got closer, I thought I spotted a couple of airships hidden under the trees, too, but in the light of dusk I couldn't really tell.

We didn't have much choice in terms of landing spots, and the only orny we had left was the two seater Eve and I had used to try and escape the pirates. Either we landed a couple of miles away and trekked in on foot, or else we rappelled down on ropes. I didn't much fancy trekking in on foot, particularly at night.

It struck me as kind of foolhardy to be heading for what was basically a thieves' hideout in the middle of the night, looking to trade our treasure for whatever food and supplies they had. But our other choice, heading overland across an entire continent, hoping not to be attacked by pirates or spotted by officials, seemed even crazier.

In the end, we parked ourselves over a clearing and waited for the locals to notice us. It didn't take long, what with the engines pounding and our ship blotting out the night sky. I sent the order down to Gigi to cut the engines, then had everyone gather in the Booty Hold, armed to the teeth with every weapon we had.

We'd dressed as disreputably as we could. If we weren't actual pirates we could at least look the part. I'd even convinced Molly to show off her prosthetics. With our hair all messed up, scary make-up splashed across our faces, clothed in leather and bristling with swords and guns, we definitely looked like a bunch of piratical women you wouldn't want to mess with.

I'd pulled my matted, tangled hair through a couple of holes I cut in an aviator cap, like dreadlocked pigtails. Otherwise I left my clothes as they were. Somebody had to look respectable enough to trade with.

I ordered the Booty Hold opened and looked down. The locals were also armed to the teeth, with everything from bows and arrows to long rifles and pistols. They looked to be from every race and background – Europans, Africers, a couple of Zhou, even a few animen.

We were about fifty feet above them. The tops of the trees brushed against the bottom of our hull. Somebody on the ground yelled something up to us in a language none of us spoke. I yelled down. "Anglic?"

"I speak Anglic, yes!" another guy yelled up. He was Europan, as scruffy looking as they come.

"We want to trade!"

"Toss down your ropes and we come up!"

I looked over to a couple of the girls and nodded. They tossed down ropes. The scruffy man said something to the others, and they grabbed the ropes and tied them to the trees. Once we were safely moored, a few men climbed up the lines.

The first one through the bay doors was a monkey animan. He barely wore any clothes, just a pair of dirty grey pants that stopped at his calves, a vest filled with pockets, and a bandoleer of pistols. Thick gold earrings pierced both his ears.

He scanned the crew with dark, intelligent eyes and spotted Gigi right away. "Sister," he said, with a nod of his simian head.

Gigi nodded back, all feline aloofness. "Brother."

The rest of the traders came aboard, each dressed as shoddily as the monkey animan, each just as armed to the teeth.

I stepped forward. "I'm Captain Sunset Val."

The scruffy man took my offered hand and shook it. "Wyss Dupree. Nice ship."

"Thanks."

"What're you after?"

"Sorry?"

"What supplies do you want?"

"Food, water, fuel. The usual. A couple of other things." I really, really hoped that my faked confident indifference would fool him.

"What've you got to offer?"

"Whatever you see in this hold."

What he saw obviously impressed him. Impressed them all, from the looks on their faces. Mrs. Shorty had outdone herself preparing everything for trade. Rugs and clothes draped every available surface. Machine parts gleamed in their open cases. And the treasures of the former crew had been placed on Argenta's old crate, a makeshift display table covered with a black cloth and placed under the overhanging lights to maximize the shiny. I'd also gotten Gigi to replace as much of the crow decorations as possible, and piled them into the inventory.

"Dunno if we can offer fair value for the trade," Dupree said, starting the negotiations.

I shrugged, as if such things were beneath the notice of a captain. "You'll have to speak to my quartermaster for that." I introduced him to Mrs. Shorty, I mean, Mrs. Throckwaddle. She inspected him with a critical eye and obviously found him lacking. As an aside, as I turned away, I said to her, "See if they have any women looking to crew."

"Plenty of slaves, if that's what you're after," Dupree offered.

I wasn't the only member of the crew who stiffened at his words. "Really."

"Sure. Don't normally trade in 'em, not much of a market out here, see, but the last ship through here wanted rid of 'em in a hurry."

"How many?"

"Two dozen, near enough."

"And the ship? Which way did she head?"

"North northwest, thereabouts. Why?"

"Just curious. Wouldn't want to run into some slavers and come up short, right?"

He gave me a odd look, then decided I must be joking around, because he started laughing. I laughed back, but there wasn't any joy in my laughter.

"Anyhow, we'll take those slaves off your hands."

"How many?"

"All of them."

This time the look he gave me was incredulous, but he recovered quick enough. "Well now, dunno 'bout that. We paid good money for 'em."

I snatched a ruby the size of my thumbnail off the display case and flicked it at him. "I'm sure we can work something out."

He caught it in one hand and stared at it for all of two seconds. Then it disappeared into a pocket and he grinned. "I'm sure we can, Captain."

In the end, Mrs. Shorty haggled us a few weeks' worth of fresh food, resupplying our water stores, two tons of coke (which sounds like a lot but wasn't really), a orny and a half (which Gigi insisted we'd need for parts), and every slave they had. The crew managed to get themselves some fine clothes from our stores before we flew in to Djen, so we weren't hurting there, and Mrs. Shorty kept more than enough for the new girls. Weapons, we'd need, though, so a lot of Captain Crow's treasure trove went into getting swords and guns enough for everyone on board.

It galled me to find out Captain Crow had been right about one thing. He'd treated us well, as slaves. The girls we bought were practically starved. Several of them had been beaten. All of them were terrified of us, and none of them had more than a thin filthy shift to wear. I told Eve and her nurses to show the new girls to our dance hall, see to their injuries, get them cleaned up, get them fed. Then I sent orders down to Hilda and Brunhilde to cook up a batch of something easy to digest for the new girls to eat. All the rich pies and cakes and roasts would probably just make them sick.

The trading took most of the night, and then the unloading of our wares and loading of our purchases took the rest of the next day. Luckily the Booty Hold was so close to the launch bay for the ornies, and the launch bay had a couple of cranes that Gigi figured out how to use to move the supplies.

That was the first time I saw my ship from the ground, the first time I saw our figurehead. A blighted crow it was, carved to look like it was swooping in to rake us with its scything claws, carved to look rotting and cadaverous, painted with the entire putrescent spectrum of decay, excepting only its burning brilliant orange eyes.

I took a good long look at her from the ground, then I turned to Gigi. "Get it off my ship."

"We don't have a replacement, Captain."

"We haven't chosen a name, either. I don't care. Every second that thing hangs from our girl, it's a slap in the face to every former slave aboard her. We'll fly under no name nor figurehead rather than fly under that bastard's choices."

No one would trade for her, though. Several of the locals swore it was bad luck to fly without a figurehead, swore we'd come to no good end without one. I didn't care. I wouldn't fly with a corpse attached to the front of my ship, pirate tradition or not.

Once we'd loaded up, Dupree invited us to take a meal with him. I'd seen enough movies to expect a double-cross of some kind, so I sent our regrets and we took to the skies. When we were well under way, I went to the slave mess, where we fed our new 'purchases'.

"Any of them speak Anglic?"

Eve looked up at me from where she tended one of the new girl's bandages as the girl tried to eat. Or at least, as she played with her food.

Almost all the new girls were young, like, under twenty five. None was younger than fourteen or so. All of them seemed older when I looked them in the eye. Most of them had the yellow skin and black hair that back home I'd call Asian and here they called Zhou. Several of the others had browner skin than mine, again, with black hair. Back home I'd likely call them Middle Eastern. There were only a couple of Europans, with olive skin, dark hair and pale eyes, and a couple more Africers, with hair and skin as dark as a cup of black coffee.

"None, Captain, though some speak Atlan," Eve answered, smiling gently at the injured girl, nodding encouragement. The injured girl wouldn't meet her eyes.

"Do we have anyone on board who speaks Zhou?"

"I do, Captain," said a voice behind me.

I turned. Miss Merryweather walked up to us. She said something in not-Chinese to the injured girl, who replied quickly in the same language.

"Wow, how many languages do you speak?"

"Seven, Captain. Atlan, Anglic, Zhou, Russic, Anatol, Gallian, Bavardish. A little Levantian, but not enough to really count."

"Well Miss Merryweather, looks like you have some new students. I want everyone learning Atlan as soon as possible."

"Aye, Captain."

"Will you translate for me?"

"Of course, Captain. But to which group? Some of these unfortunates are clearly not Zhou."

"No, obviously not. Can anyone on the crew speak Saud or Levant?"

"Salia does, I believe, Captain."

"Okay, send for her, please."

While we waited for Salia to show up I watched the slaves. They were barely eating, listless and suspicious. Eve had done a good job, though. All of them had bandages over their cuts and bruises, and all of them were wearing new, clean shifts. We'd let them choose their own clothing after their meal.

Salia showed up and I asked her to translate for me. She said her Saud was pretty rusty, since she'd been raised in Hispania, but she'd try.

I stood on a chair and waved my arms for their attention.

"Ladies, welcome." I waited for Miss Merryweather and Salia to translate. "You were taken by slavers and sold to thieves. So were we. But we rose up against our pirate captors. And now we have rescued you from a lifetime of servitude. You are free!"

At first the words didn't seem to sink in. They looked at us suspiciously. Then disbelief and anger flitted across their faces, a sort of how dare you toy with us like this? And then, finally, it sank in. They were free.

Some of them cheered. Some of them cried. Some of them hugged each other.

And once that series of reactions was over, the whirlwind of questions. Yes, they were free to leave us at the next port. Yes, they could join our crew if they'd rather. Yes, we would give them clothes and food. No, they wouldn't be forced to become pirates. No, we couldn't do anything about the slave brand they all wore.

That's when my heart was replaced with a burning coal of fury. Seeing the brand that had been seared into their flesh.

A mermaid.

In my mind, there was no doubt. The ship that we'd outrun had taken these women as slaves. Before or after our encounter, I don't know. But we could have helped them, one way or another, if I'd been brave enough, a good enough leader, to confront the mermaid ship, which the Saud called The Syren.

I offered the women a chance for revenge. We would hunt down The Syren, board her, take her, make the pirates aboard pay for their crimes.

Chapter Twenty Nine

The Daily Life of a Pirate Captain Isn't What I Expected

It was amazingly difficult to find a single ship in all the skies.

For a week we hunted, flying up and down the Afric coast. During that time, we learned Atlan and swordfighting. With so many people not speaking the same language, we sort of started developing our own, a mix of Anglic and Atlan, Zhou and Afric, Gallic and Bavardish and a little of everything. Miss Merryweather worked us pretty hard to learn Atlan, but the shipspeak we came up with started taking over.

Almost all of the new girls voted to stay on board, once we explained to them how voting worked. Again, I was amazed that the very idea of making up their own minds had never been explained to them. Even though they hadn't been branded, in a very real way, these girls had been slaves their whole lives. Slaves to the sexist society they grew up in.

Two of the new girls tried to kill themselves. Something about the dishonour of being a slave, even for a few days. We managed to get to them in time, and Eve patched them up. I gave them both to Molly to train, hoping some of her hate and determination for revenge would rub off on them.

And beyond that excitement, the week passed in incredible boredom. Two or three hours of Atlan lessons, two or three hours of swordfighting, was a little like being back in school. On top of which, I had to be the captain of the ship. I had to make sure everyone had something to do, and that everyone with something to do was doing it. I had to make every decision with regards to our direction, which way, how far, how high, how long. I had to make sure everyone had enough to eat and drink, had a place to sleep, had clothes to wear. I had to deal with engine problems, not with our still unnamed ship, but with the orny we'd traded for that Gigi had insisted she could get running.

A lot of the time it was a simple matter of letting the person with the problem explain the problem, then offer me a solution (often at my prompting), and then tell them to do what they'd just suggested they do. It boiled down to responsibility. None of them wanted to be responsible for a decision. They wanted me to be the responsible one. So I took the responsibility from them, and the ship managed to work well.

The only real surprise during that week came from the new girls. All of the Afric and Saud girls leapt at the chance to learn swordfighting, but none of the Zhou would.

"They believe that touching a sword will render them infertile," Miss Merryweather translated. "They believe it is their... hmm. Imperative? Forgive me, Captain, I'm unsure of this word." She switched into Zhou, asking for clarification. The tall Zhou girl with long straight hair named Tring who had sort of become the spokeswoman for their group explained, head held high and proud, looking me in the eye the whole time.

When she finished, Miss Merryweather explained. "They believe the spirit of the sword will enter them and destroy? Combat? Fight with any future husband's, ahem, 'sword', preventing him from impregnating them. And that it is their duty to keep themselves ready to have as many children as possible. The number of children a Zhou woman has determines her worth in her husband's eyes."

"That's ridiculous."

"It stems from the long rivalry between Zhou and Atlan. Many warriors are needed to keep Atlan forces from taking the Zhou principalities as their own. And despite a century of cease fire, skirmishes along the border claim many lives every year, on both sides."

"So women are just what, baby factories? Ask her."

Miss Merryweather asked, and Tring answered.

"Some women choose the way of the warrior, but none will take up the sword."

"How does that work?"

"Poles, clubs, in some cases axes. But most choose the. Hmm."

"What?"

Miss Merryweather again switched into Zhou, asking a lot of questions. Tring answered them at length, turning to Miss Merryweather and demonstrating with elegant, graceful hand gestures. I felt completely forgotten, left out of the loop and ignored.

Eventually, impatience got the better of me. "Well?"

"Forgive me, Captain. She explains that it is seldom spoken of amongst non-Zhou. It is a method of fighting called the Gentle Path, or the Open Hand. The terms seem interchangeable. The Zhou have a method of fighting that involves no weapons. How fascinating."

Like karate or kung fu! "Do any of them know the Gentle Path? Ask her."

Miss Merryweather asked, and Tring answered: she did.

"Will she teach us?"

"She says she will not teach non-Zhou."

"Why not?"

"It is forbidden."

"By who?"

"The Masters of the Open Hand."

"Tell her I'm the captain of this ship, and I un-forbid them."

"She says no captain of any vessel outranks the Masters of the Open Hand."

I resisted the urge to growl. "We'll just see about that. No, don't translate. Ask her if she will teach the other Zhou, at least."

Tring reluctantly agreed to teach the other Zhou, but only those who wanted to learn.

"Well, if they won't take up the sword, and they won't learn the Gentle Path, they've got to learn to fight somehow. What about poles or axes?"

"Some of them refuse to learn to fight, Captain. They consider it. Hmm. Unclean?"

I wanted to order them to learn. I wanted to make them see how stupid they were being. I wanted a lot of things. Instead, I explained to Tring, through Miss Merryweather, that everyone aboard my ship had to help out somehow. We didn't have food enough or place aboard for women looking for a pleasure cruise. And that once we found the pirates who'd taken them as slaves, they'd all have to help take their ship. We couldn't risk our ship being taken by a more experienced crew of pirates. Either they'd fight, or they'd have to guard our vessel.

Tring told me she'd try to convince them, but didn't sound very convinced herself.

Aside from trying to make warriors out of a bunch of women who had no inclination to war, I found myself worrying more and more about supplies. I couldn't believe how fast we ran out of food. I even ordered Brunhilde and Hilda to cut rations, be less fancy, make simpler meals that would feed more people, and still we were running out of food at an alarming rate. Here I was, a pirate with an airship of my own, flying through the skies, and my biggest worry was how to keep my crew fed. It was so boringly normal.

That's what finally truly convinced me everything that was happening was really, truly real. Part of my brain held on to the idea that I was lying in a coma in a hospital somewhere back home, having been hit on the head by the exploding street lamp in the parking lot after my fencing lesson. But there was no way I would dream up something as tiresome as figuring out how to keep forty women eating three square meals a day. No, my imagination was better than that. I would be dreaming something exciting.

But pretty soon, we got all the excitement I could have dreamed up, more than enough to offset the boredom of the previous week.

Chapter Thirty

Our Foe Finally Found

Day and night, I'd kept lookouts on deck, sweeping the skies with all the goggles and binoculars and telescopes we had, trying to spot any ship at all. Turned out to be pretty much nothing in the Afric skies. The bright blue of the desert sky would have revealed any ship in hundreds of miles in every direction. Same with the skies over the sea, but there we had a lot more clouds for our quarry to hide in.

Which isn't to say we never found any ships. There were plenty of ships in the air. Just not the one we were looking for. But finally one of the girls came running up to me, and in the part-Atlan, part-Anglic, part-other language we'd been using more often than not on the ship, she explained that someone had seen something.

By then I'd grown accustomed to false alarms, but something in the girl's frantic excitement caught hold of me, and I wound up racing her topside, beating her by only the narrowest of margins. Life aboard ship had toughened me some, starting with the week I spent stoking, so the race up three flights of stairs and across the deck hadn't even winded me.

A crowd of girls stood near the rail, binoculars and telescopes and goggles all pointing the same direction. An excited babble of voices all chattering away in our shipspeak greeted me, and when they realized I'd joined them, their voices rose in excitement, volume and pitch.

"Girls! Girls! Where's this ship?" I asked in shipspeak.

As one they pointed off starboard, about thirty degrees from the bow and ten degrees below our plane. Viola turned out to be the girl who'd first spotted it, and I pushed my way through the crowd to stand beside her.

I slipped my goggles down over my eyes and resolved the lenses, turning their housings until the ship came into focus. A blurry dot off in the sky clicked, clicked, clicked into a ship.

A ship with a mermaid figurehead.

I didn't take my eyes off her. "Somebody get Gigi."

We'd come up with a plan as we'd hunted. A plan to get the ship in as close as possible, since we had only one pilot for the two ornies we had, and that was Eve. She'd have to train someone on the other as soon as we had a chance.

What we had no one trained to do was operate our cannons. There was an entire deck of cannons sitting just below the crew quarters, and not a single woman aboard ship knew how to load or fire them. I wouldn't risk anyone's lives by experimenting with them, so they pretty much sat there gathering dust.

But Gigi figured out a way for us to open the gun ports and move the unloaded cannons into position, so that it looked like we knew what we were doing. And thanks to the system of levers and pulleys and ropes and such that she worked out, it would only take a couple of women to operate.

Gigi joined me topside and looked at the ship, clicking the lenses of her goggles back and forth, back and forth, eyes narrowed in deep concentration. Her sandy little tongue slipped out of her mouth and ran back and forth across her furry lips. Her tail twitched and her hands on the rail clenched, her long claws extending.

"It's her," she said at last. "I'd swear it."

I turned to the girls. "Battle stations!"

They ran off, getting into position and spreading the word. The metal gangplanks and catwalks rattled with the thunder of booted feet hurrying throughout the ship. Once we'd come up with the plan, we'd drilled each girl until she knew exactly what to do and where to go. Every girl knew their part to play.

I slid down the handrails of the stairwells and pushed through crowds of crew on my way to the wheelhouse. "Argenta, tight to port."

Our automaidon pilot spun the wheel and the ship began to list to port, turning in a tight circle.

Then yellowish white smoke billowed out our twin smokestacks at the very rear of the ship. As we pulled into our own wake, the stink was incredible. I'd ordered every last bit of garbage thrown into the boiler furnaces, despite Gigi's insistence that it might clog up the works. I wanted our predator to think we were crippled, a lame duck, flying bait waiting to be plucked from the sky.

The Syren drew closer and closer as we spun in place, flashing us incomprehensibly. I swore that if this trick worked and we survived to get to port, I'd hire on the first airship sailor who spoke flashy. But until then, we just had to ignore her.

Outside, the sun set. Perfect timing. I ordered the ship's lights out, giving the impression we were running out of power. Then I cranked the dial to 'All Stop' myself. Without me needing to tell her, Viola went off to pass the word for silent running.

We settled in the relatively windless air, surrounded by a reeking cloud of our own filth.

The ship drew closer, closer. I kept it in view, and ordered, "Get Serena up."

Domina ran off to deliver my order. Another thing we'd need to figure out would be some kind of intercom or something. But, first things first, Val. Survive attacking a pirate ship filled with desperate slavers before you go inventing radio or whatever.

The waiting was killing me. I ordered the bridge cleared, even Argenta. I'd need her fearsome fighting skills tonight.

Spotlights ran along our side as the Syren inspected us for survivors, looking through portholes and windows. Every girl aboard knew well enough to keep hidden. My heart pounded and a trickle of sweat went down my back as I crouched low in the shadows of the wheelhouse, waiting for the light to pass through, see the wheelhouse was empty, then move on.

We couldn't take them, not in a one-on-one cannon battle. Our only hope of defeating them lay in convincing them to come aboard and search for survivors.

A voice outside, distorted by a brass loudspeaking cone, called for any survivors to show themselves in Atlan, then again in Gallic and Afric. I finally understood enough Atlan, and Gallic was close enough to French, that I could guess they'd said the same in Afric.

Our three decoys went topside, waving white towels and shirts to show they were unarmed. Molly led them. She was easily the fiercest looking of us all. Eve might have looked scarier, but we couldn't count on her acting abilities. She was just too nice and polite. Except when the Doc died, then she kind of She-Hulked out. Anyway, Molly was in the lead. The other two girls were Viola and a curvy redhead named Ginger Cherry, and I swear I'm not making that up. They were easily the two prettiest girls we had aboard ship. We'd tarted them up as best we could, hoping to use their feminine charms distract any pirates who boarded us. Hilda had volunteered to be a decoy as well. She was pretty enough and had more than enough 'charms' to distract any pirates who would be lured aboard, but when Brunhilde found out her daughter would be dressed up (or down, depending on your point of view) like a pleasure girl, her mother instincts came out, she put her foot down, and that was that. Hilda pouted for a day, then I found her something else to do in my master plan.

I crept out of the wheelhouse and down to the nearly empty Booty Hold. The orny lay nestled in the crane cradle, ready for launch. Eve lay in the pilot's seat, hidden under a tarp that would whisk away once the launch bay doors opened.

I checked my guns, making sure they were fully loaded, hoping I wouldn't have to use them. I didn't want to kill anyone, not really, but I knew plenty of the women aboard would be more than willing to slaughter slavers all night. Each had their reasons. Dead husbands, dead boyfriends, dead brothers and fathers and sons. Their lives ruined by the slave mark on their arm. Molly's arm and leg and eye.

Me, I'd been yanked here by a mad scientist. Pirates had destroyed my only chance to get home when they'd destroyed Doc's dirigible. I didn't really have a life here to be ruined by pirate slavers, so I didn't especially have a huge hate for their kind, beyond a sort of righteous fury that burned at the back of my heart, that women would be so sorely treated. That was wrong, a wrong I could combat. And combating that wrong required this ruse, sanctioned the slaughter.

Okay, yes, I was a little alliterative. Again.

Seeing Eve in place and checking the launch bay door switch a tenth time, I moved as silently as I could through the ship, making sure the other girls were in position. Everyone was ready.

I heard booted heels on the topdeck, heavier than any of the girls we'd sent as decoys. The pirates had boarded us.

Chapter Thirty One

Springing the Trap

That was the worst part, waiting as they boarded us, clomping around topside, looking for any sign of a trap. What happened after happened so fast it was hard to be scared or even to think much about it at the time. Molly fed them the story we'd come up with, a tale of woe as the crew took ill, one by one, until all that were left were Molly and two pleasure girls. As a member of the crew, Molly knew a little about running the ship but obviously not enough, and the pleasure girls were pretty much useless in an emergency like this.

We'd debated the idea of using a mysterious disease as the reason why there were no crew left. Serena thought it might scare them off, make them abandon ship and blast us out of the sky from a safe distance. Molly said only the blight would scare off hardened slavers. There was also the risk that they'd take our decoys aboard their ship as slaves without checking below decks, and then we'd have to board the Syren to get them back.

Molly knew how to get them belowdecks, though. In a hushed voice, she promised them a hidden treasure, one only she knew how to find. Though I had been sceptical, it worked like a charm. The lure of getting their hands on the ship's wealth before their comrades aboard the Syren proved enough to get them to follow Molly.

She led them right into our trap, of course. In the slave quarters turned dance hall turned crew quarters, a group of highly motivated and very armed women waited to exact some revenge.

"No tricks, now," one of the slavers said as they passed my hiding spot. He grabbed Ginger by the waist and raised his dagger to point at her stomach. "Or this plump pigeon gets it in the gut."

Ginger simpered admirably, begging him not to hurt her, promising him a world of delights the likes of which he'd only ever dreamed of. From his bent, broken nose to his missing teeth to his bow-legged gait and especially the hungry look in his eyes, I guessed he'd never really experienced a world of delights with a willing woman. He actually licked his lips.

"No tricks," Molly agreed, leading the way into the trap. "Through here."

She nearly gave it away right then. A little of her hate slipped through in her tone, teeth clenched with bloodthirsty vengeance so close at hand. The bow-legged slaver stopped, suspicious. The other slavers stopped with him.

There were nearly a dozen or so, all human except for one animan, a frog-faced man with skin that was fish-belly white and nearly no clothes on. I would have to say the blend of mammal and amphibian definitely favoured the mammal side in this guy. Maybe non-mammal animen were less viable, I don't know.

From my hiding place I saw Molly nearly lose it, her human hand balling into a fist and back, itching to pull the dagger she had hidden in her sleeve. "Just inside, sir. Not far now."

He didn't like it, not one bit. Even from where I hid I could tell.

The open door beckoned. Molly stepped through, disappearing into darkness. Bowlegs jerked his head toward the door, and the frogman jumped through. The other pirates followed. One dragged Viola by the arm.

Bowlegs shoved Ginger up against the wall. "I'll just stay with pigeon here. She can stay showing me them delights what she promised."

The other pirates laughed roughly. Ginger played along, pretending to be eager to please him, if only to save her own skin.

Now if the trap sprung shut, Ginger would be killed and Bowlegs would raise the alarm. And if the door didn't close, the noise from our attacks would raise the alarm for us. And there was no treasure in that room, so in a few seconds we'd be found out, anyway.

I didn't have any choice. I pulled off my boots. Bowlegs leaned in close to Ginger, using his knife to slit the laces of her corset. She laughed it off, like it was some kind of sexy game. Barefoot, I crept silently from my hiding place. While he was distracted, drooling over her cleavage, she spotted me and made a 'do something hurry!' face at me.

I pulled out my knife, spun my finger in the air to get her to turn him around. She grabbed his head and forced his face into her cleavage, closing her eyes in revulsion as she manoeuvred him around. She made sounds of pleasure as I crept toward them.

This wasn't killing in the heat of battle, or trying to save my own life. This was murder, pure and simple. I told myself that if I didn't kill him we were all dead, that it was for the good of everyone that he had to die. It didn't make it easier, but I sank the blade into him all the same.

Serena had shown me where to stab a man. Not in the back, not in the side. Both were wounds a man could walk away from. Too much bone to go through in the upper back, not enough important bits in the lower back. Too much gut meat in the sides. Oh, he would die from a wound like that, but not before he killed Ginger or raised the alarm. Or both.

Ginger pushed him away, and I stabbed him in the throat. Not once but three times in rapid succession. His blood sprayed in a wide arc that got Ginger and I both, hot and slick and wet. He dropped his knife with a clatter that I swore echoed through the ship.

We lowered him to the ground as he choked and clawed at his ragged throat, gouts of blood pumping through his clenched fingers. His booted heels drummed against the floor, beating out his death knell.

"Everything alright, Tom?" a rough voice called from the room. "You need help with that pigeon?"

Ginger yelled out in ecstasy, covering the sound of Bowlegs' gurgled choking. Unpleasant laughter came from the open doorway.

I wiped tears from my cheeks, not sure when they'd spilled. A bright ball of fury bloomed beneath my beating heart, brilliant and blinding. I got to my feet and ran to the door.

"NOW!"

Ginger slammed the door shut behind her and the killing started. It was messy and brutal and desperate. Serena and Argenta and Gigi and all our best swordswomen were there, and Molly and Viola and me. But the pirates somehow had known they were walking into a trap, because they all drew pistols and the echoing boom of so many guns in a tight enclosed place going off in rapid fire soon deafened us. We dove for cover. Some of the girls weren't as lucky as me. Some trick of acoustics or imagination provided in crystal clarity the thick meaty sound of bullets slamming into their flesh, the terrible high wail of their shrieks of pain, the panting sobs as their life bled out of them.

Through the thick blue grey haze of gun smoke I saw the pirates huddled together, back to back. I watched from where I hid until they ran out of bullets. Then I ordered the attack.

Most of my girls jumped up from their hiding spots, knives and swords at the ready. Most, but not all. I saw Viola on the floor, squeezing her leg to keep the blood from escaping, teeth gritted against the pain. I pulled out a pistol and fired at the pirates. It was hard to miss, they were packed together so tight. I fired again and again until my pistol was empty, then drew my sword and joined the melee.

In the cramped quarters, we took our revenge on them. We killed and were killed. It was a nightmare of blood-slicked floors, screams of the dying, flashing blades and booming gunfire. Argenta saved my life more than once, and at one point I found myself back to back with Serena.

That was the only good memory I have of the fight. She and I moved together, as one, like dancers. I'd parry a blow aimed at her, she'd riposte one aimed at me. We turned in place, taking on six of the slavers at once, until our girls got behind them, back-stabbed them, hamstrung them, gutted them as they fell.

In the end, the frogman was the hardest to kill. He and Gigi kept chasing each other around the room, her powerful cat musculature propelling her in leaps that were almost good enough, high enough, fast enough to catch his amphibian frame. I grabbed a gun and fired, got lucky, watched him fall. Then Gigi was on him, all claws and snarls. When she finished he looked like he'd been through a blender.

Four of our girls died, including Viola. She bled out so quick there was nothing we could do. Another five were too wounded to continue. Somehow I managed to get through it without a scratch. It didn't seem fair.

Of course, we should have known it wouldn't be as easy as that. Their friends aboard the Syren had heard the gunfire and come looking for trouble. The rest of my women were more than willing to give them all the trouble they could handle, but it was still a near thing. If I survived, I promised myself that the next ship we took would be so full of cannonshot that there wouldn't be anyone left to board us. You know, once we found someone who knew how to load and fire a cannon.

We fought hard. My girls wanted vengeance so bad, so terribly, that it reminded me of the ancient Greek myths of the Furies, the goddesses of holy retribution. Terrible to behold, they laid into the slavers with an almost mindless desire to slaughter them all.

And it was a slaughter. Most of the slavers had never seen women so fierce, so determined to kill, like all the repression of living in their sexist, racist society had been let loose. For a time, that fierce determination carried us through them, surprised the slavers and caught them off guard. When it became clear they were fighting for their lives, against a foe that seemed not to care if they lived or died, then our fight came much, much harder.

Somehow I wound up in the launch bay with a half dozen women, looking for more slavers. The bay doors were open. Eve had launched the orny. It reminded me that we had a plan, not just mindless slaughtering.

"To the topdeck!"

I led the way up stairwells, gathering more girls as we went, fighting when we had to, running if we didn't, pausing only to reload our pistols whenever we came to one of the caches I'd ordered hidden around the ship. We charged onto the topdeck and saw the Syren.

"Now, now, the guns!"

My order was passed back, and our gun ports opened as one. Cannons pulled themselves into position, thanks to Gigi's marvellous mechanical manipulations.

I grabbed the loudspeaker cone and held it up. "Surrender now or we blow you from the sky!"

That was about when the pirates aboard our ship made it onto the topdeck. The fighting raged hard and bloody. Screams of pain and shrieks of outrage and angry curses filled the air.

Then Tring's Zhou finally joined the fight, armed with nothing but their hands.

Their Open Hands.

They laid into the slavers, two or three jumping one slaver at a time, disarming him, breaking bones, beating him bloody, then moving on to the next, and the next after that.

Some of the slavers saw how it was going and made to get back to their ship. High above us, our balloons were so close they bumped against each other. Crossing from ship to ship required swinging across on ropes, which some of the slavers readily did. I saw one misjudge his jump and slip off the rope, plummeting hundreds of feet to his death.

We had practised swinging on ropes on our still unnamed ship, practised until our hands were raw from rope burn. Crossing from ours to theirs should have been easy enough, but seeing their guy slip and fall reminded everyone of the inherent danger.

I grabbed a rope, stood on the railing and tried to think of something inspirational to say, tried to think of anything except the hundreds of feet of night sky between me and a sudden painful stop. No words came to me (I know, shock!) so I hoped my actions would speak for themselves. In the end I just jumped, and hoped.

The deck of the Syren rushed at me and I almost didn't let go of the rope in time. As it was I landed painfully on my behind. Serena, of course, landed with perfect, flawless grace, then helped me to my feet.

"Thanks."

"You're velcome. There are more of them than ve expected, yes?"

"Yes. We should just blow her and run."

"Vhat if she has more slaves?"

"Yeah, I know. Okay, come on."

"Go time?"

The expression from my world sounded odd coming from her. I grinned. "Yeah. Go time."

We helped the other girls as they swung aboard. It amazed me that we weren't being met with any opposition. Amazed me, and made me suspicious.

"Careful, girls. They could have a trap waiting for us, just like we had for them."

"Let us spring it, then," Molly said savagely.

We went below decks.

Chapter Thirty Two

Death and Disappointment

Of course it was a trap. The Syren was a smaller ship, with less places to hide, but hide the slavers did, in their mess hall. I sent a gang of girls to take the engine room, and Molly and another gang to capture the wheelhouse. It left me with Serena and a half dozen women, all eager for a fight. We went looking for more slavers, and Serena said she could smell them in the mess hall.

I've seen enough cop shows and war movies to know how to go into a tight situation. Two of my biggest girls kicked the doors open, we rushed in, crouching low to keep from being shot, guns blazing. I'd shown my girls how to do that much.

It wasn't pretty. Ginger got shot and went down screaming. I felt something tug at my sleeve, looked around, saw no one close. Later I'd find a bullet hole clear through the sleeve. Right then, I didn't care. I emptied my pistols into the room, not really aiming, and drew my sword.

In the end, there were just too many of them. The Syren had absolutely not followed the same crewing policies as Captain Crow's Carrion. They believed in the 'many pirates make light work' motto of piracy and slaving. But what really surprised me and caught me off guard? Was a certain one-eyed bastard named Tyr Ebonfury. Out of nowhere during the fight, he showed up with an evil, hungry grin on his face and a sword in each hand. It was like a nightmare come true. One second I fought against some random slaver, the next there were whirling blades levelled at my face and Serena by my side and one-eyed vengeance come back to haunt me.

He was too good. It was all I could do to keep him from skewering me, parrying his blows as he jabbed and slashed and jabbed again, almost too fast to follow. Serena was everywhere at once, blocking and parrying and occasionally riposting, but he backed us into a corner and I could barely keep up. Out of my peripheral vision I saw my girls going down, overpowered, overwhelmed, captured and beaten.

The attack was over soon enough. Our plans had failed.

Chapter Thirty Three

An Unwelcome Surprise Has Unfortunate Consequences

They disarmed us, rounded us up topside, tied together. The dead were tossed overboard. I cried, and I wasn't the only one. Dr. Enerva, that blonde evil bitch, inspected the wounded with a hungry, joyous, insane eye. She'd have more than enough subjects for her experiments for months to come. Molly kept shrieking the vilest things you can imagine at Enerva, until finally one of the crew stuffed a rag in Molly's mouth. Even that wasn't enough to calm her down, so one of them clubbed her in the back of the head and knocked her out.

Tyr Ebonfury came and stood in front of me, smirking.

I had to ask. "How did you even get on this ship?"

He laughed. "Captain Crow and Captain Caliper have had a long partnership of watching each other's backs."

"Captain Who?"

"Captain Me," said a deep voice. A huge man with dark hair, a huge bushy beard, and one eye stepped forward. Well, one real eye and one artificial eye, like Molly's. He leaned down to face me, and the eyelens twisted, focussing on me. He had a couple of missing teeth and his breath reeked strongly of garlic and fish. "Sunset Val, eh? Come from another world to cause us all so much trouble."

My guts turned to ice. "How did you know that?"

"Ah, well, that would be my fault, I'm afraid."

And that's when I got the other surprise that floored me completely.

Dr. Sweetwater stepped out of the crowd of slavers, alive and apparently well.

"Doc?! What? How? You died!"

"All evidence to the contrary, of course," he smiled at me. "I apologize for the ruse, my dear, but you see the fact of the matter is that the entire event was staged."

"I don't understand. Staged for who?"

Captain Caliper laughed. "Go on, Monty. Explain it to her. Use words everyone can understand."

A flash of annoyance crossed the Doc's face, but he forced a smile at the Captain. "You see, my experiments in alternative sciences were not entirely sanctioned by the Atlan authorities. None of my radical theories found any official channels of funding, and so for the most part I was forced to fund my research with my own fortune. Those meagre funds ran out some years ago, and so I turned to investors. My reputation by then was somewhat tarnished by jealous competitors, and respectable investors would not even reply to my inquiries to meet. It was in a moment of desperation that I went seeking the solace of spirits, and in turn coincidence led me to encounter a former colleague from my collegiate days of yore."

"That would be me," Captain Caliper said. "I'd studied at the same school with Monty before being kicked out for grave robbery. Honestly, where they imagine a student will find the funds to pay for prime legal bodies to experiment on is beyond me."

"Caliper had turned to piracy, and offered to fund my experiments. In exchange I would supply him with equipment, whatever findings my own research led to, and design weapons for his use."

"I was never much for machines, but Monty knew his way through them inside and out."

"Nonsense, you simply never applied yourself. You would have made a fine scientist, had you eluded capture long enough to graduate."

"Bah, why waste my time when I can get a genius such as yourself to do the work for me?"

I rolled my eyes. "I hate to interrupt your mutual admiration society, but how exactly does any of this have anything to do with me?"

Caliper sniffed distastefully. "Oh, well, you see, lately there have been rumblings about Atlan abolishing slavery, and rescinding all letters of marque."

"It would be frightfully unprofitable to allow that to happen, of course. Not to mention the loss to the world of science," Doc added. "My research would end, as would Dr. Enerva's incredible discoveries in the field of biomechanical interfaces."

She disengaged herself from Tyr's embrace and gave Doc a little nod. "Thank you for that, Doctor."

"Not at all, Doctor. Credit where it's due, and all that."

Yeah, they really loved complimenting each other. What, and also ever.

Doc turned back to me. "Naturally the actions of a few scientists, slavers, and pirates would have no effect whatsoever on the political climate or the machinations of the authorities. Not even a pirate with so influential a politician as the Minister of Ys on his side. So we sought new territories to exploit.

"At first we thought only of this world. But then it occurred to me, what if there were other worlds? What if we could travel back and forth, as easily as stepping through a doorway?"

I remembered the blinding light, the crackling electricity, the terrible terrifying trip from my world to this, and found his analogy lacking. "And what, plunder my world? We have weapons you couldn't even imagine. Your little ship wouldn't last a day there."

Captain Caliper, Tyr, and even Doc Sweetwater laughed.

"Who ever said anything about travelling to your world?" Caliper asked. "There are multitudes of worlds, lying ready and waiting for us to pillage and plunder to our hearts' content!"

I hadn't thought of that. "Besides, all of Doc's stuff was lost in that storm. Oh, that was all staged, too. I get it. So, what? The Syren was waiting in the storm cloud to offload the Doc's equipment as Eve and I tried to escape from the slavers?"

"I told you she had a remarkable intellect," Doc said. Tyr grunted in disgust.

I smirked my cheekiest smirk at him. "Smart enough to outwit you and that joke of a captain, Crow." He ground his teeth in anger, grimacing at the memory. I laughed. "Yeah, that's right, a little girl led a bunch of slaves and chased you off your own ship. Wow, you really do suck, don't you?"

He jumped toward me, restrained only by Captain Caliper's meaty hand.

"Wal," Serena warned. Maybe I was pushing him too much, but I'd had enough.

"Enough's enough," I said loud and clear.

Molly sat up. Whatever Enerva had done to her head to connect the eyelens to her brain had made her skull really hard. Probably a metal plate or whatever to replace the bone that had been removed to make way for the wires and electronics implanted in there. Anyhow, she had faked being knocked out the whole time.

She flexed her prosthetic arm and burst apart the ropes holding her captive, then opened a compartment on her forearm that Gigi had installed. Molly raised her arm and a rocket flew straight at Dr. Enerva, who managed to dodge out of the way, or else Tyr pushed her. I couldn't tell from where I stood. The rocket flew off into the night sky, then exploded in a brilliant flare.

"You missed," Tyr spat at Molly as six or seven crew jumped her and wrestled her to the ground.

"And what are you smiling about?" Caliper asked me.

I grinned at him. "See, here's the thing. I knew we didn't have much of a chance against a crew of hardened pirates. Experienced slavers against barely trained slaves? No contest, not in open combat."

He sneered at me. "You led them to their deaths."

"No, see, I knew we didn't have a chance. So I planned it that way."

His sneer disappeared. "What?"

"I planned it that way. I knew you wouldn't be fooled by our empty cannons. No one would fire on an airship at this close proximity, both vessels would be destroyed. Molly explained that one to me."

From where she lay on the topdeck, her face a bloody mess, she smiled fiercely at me.

"I knew we'd have to come aboard. I knew we'd walk into a trap. I even knew we'd likely be captured." I shrugged. "I couldn't plan on everything, though. I didn't expect Tyr and his psycho bitch to be aboard. I didn't think Doc Sweetwater would turn out to be alive, or that he'd be pure loco in the cabeza." That got a lot of blank looks, so I explained. "You, know, nuts. Cuckoo. Insane in the brain. Mad."

"You mustn't call me mad," Doc said, his hand visibly trembling as he raised it to his head.

"Or what? You'll yank me from my world, give me up to slavers, abandon me to a life of pain and humiliation and an early death of debilitating disease, if I'm lucky? Oh no, not that." I gave him my best in your face grin. "Mad, mad, mad as a hatter, mad mad mad. What are you going to do about it?"

His eye was twitching and the veins in his forehead stood out in the light cast from the electric lamps in the ship's rigging. "Stop it. You mustn't call me mad!"

My grin disappeared, replaced with white-hot fury. "You're. CRAZY!"

His hand whipped out and he backhanded me across the face. I'd seen it coming, and tried to roll with it, but he still slapped me hard enough that he split my lip and blood trickled down my chin. His upper lip peeled away from his teeth in an angry snarl and he grabbed me by the jaw, forcing his face close to mine.

Nothing sane stared through his glassy eyes. No shred of reason remained. His voice, when he spoke, was quiet and still and flat, as if even emotion had fled this display. "You'll see how mad I can be."

I just smiled. "Bring it, psycho."

He snarled incoherently and began untying me from the others when a pirate ran up to the Captain.

"Captain, we're losing altitude!" he reported.

"What? How?"

I'd kept everyone's attention on me and the Doc as behind their backs our nameless ship started rising away. Or more accurately, we'd begun sinking. The rocket had done its job.

Notifying Eve that we were ready for her part of the plan, that is.

Chapter Thirty Four

More Twists Than a Corkscrew's Shadow

A lot of things happened at once just then. Captain Caliper started barking orders, and his crew rushed to comply. At sea, a sinking ship meant rushing to bail out the water, or failing that, all hands on deck, abandon ship, get in the lifeboats and hope someone finds you before the freezing water or the sharks kill you. I'd seen Titanic, and even Jaws. I knew what was what.

In an airship, though, it meant a long slow drop. Time enough to maybe find the problem and fix it. Time enough to maybe save the ship, and their lives. Only, I knew they weren't going to find it in time.

While the crew scrambled into the rigging, Tring and her girls rappelled down to the topdeck.

Wait, let me back up.

When I led my women aboard the Syren by way of swinging from ropes, Eve had ferried Tring and her girls across by way of ornithopter. Not onto the topdeck, even though we'd needed every hand we had, even Open Hands, in the fight in the mess hall. No, Eve took Tring's Zhou onto the Syren's balloon, where they waited for Molly's rocket flare, which in turn signalled Eve and Tring to burst their balloon.

See, Gigi had explained to me how airship balloons were built. The balloon they all hung from was actually a giant framework with an outer protective sheath built around what she called, and don't laugh, a bladder, filled with some lighter than air gas like helium or hydrogen.

Eve had landed our orny on top of the Syren's balloon. Tring and her girls had tied it in place to keep it from falling off, then they'd gotten to work. When the rocket had flared, they cut open the outer sheath and slipped into the framework, piercing small holes in the bladder. Seems their aversion to swords didn't extend to cooking knives, which were just big enough to pierce the heavy canvas of the sheath and the thick rubberised silk that made up the bladder. Not enough to make it burst and blow up like that Hindenburg from olden days back home, but just enough that the lighter than air gas would leak out slowly. All they had to do was be careful not to make any sparks on their way out, or we'd all be roasted in a giant fireball.

Then they rappelled down the ropes Eve had brought along in the second seat of the orny, landing on the topdeck just as all chaos was let loose from Captain Caliper's orders.

See? Doc Sweetwater was right. I do have a remarkable intellect.

So where was I? Oh right. Tring and her girls swung down and let us loose, ripping into the pirates scrambling around, disarming the ones they could, disabling the ones they couldn't. Me and my girls, we grabbed the disarmed arms and set our sights on slaughter, wreaked righteous revenge, and unfettered female fury.

Was I worried about plummeting to our dooms? Not as much as getting my hands on Doc Sweetwater. We all had people on this ship we wanted to make pay, and pay dearly. I spotted Molly chasing down Dr. Enerva, limping bloodily along, mechanical fist clenching and unclenching in spasmodic rage. Tring and her girls were just tearing Caliper's crew to pieces. Serena and Tyr faced off once more, swords flashing so quickly they were almost invisible.

I found Doc Sweetwater belowdecks, scrambling over crates covered by tarps, digging through piles and piles of equipment, trying to decide what to save and what to leave behind.

"Why, Doc? Tell me why!"

He whirled around, eyes wild with madness. "Why? Science, of course! To have my name writ large in the annals of history, the greatest scientist that ever lived!"

"Right. Wow. I really didn't know the half of it before. You're willing to let a bunch of slavers and pirates have access to other worlds to rape and plunder to their heart's content so long as you get famous for it? And somehow you insist you're not mad."

"I! AM! NOT! MAD!" he shrieked, spittle flying from his lips.

He attacked me with a wrench. I parried and riposted, disarming him easily. The wrench flew through a window with a crash.

We circled around each other. I didn't want to kill him. After all, he was the only person who could send me home.

The ship tipped forward into a nosedive as the air pressure in the ship's bladder decreased. Equipment and crates began to shift and slide along the floor, catching up against the wall, the windows. Some smaller pieces fell out the broken window, spiralling away into darkness.

"Everything would have been fine if only you'd not been such a blasted troublemaker," Doc said. He picked up a gear and threw it at me.

I knocked it out of the way with my sword. "Don't break your arm patting yourself on the back, Doc. Your plan had more holes in it than the ship's bladder has now. Like, how were you going to get an entire ship through a street light?"

"What does a street lamp have anything to do with my aetheric portal?"

"What portal?"

"This portal." He caressed a large metal crate lovingly. My frenzied brain noticed it had brass fittings, setting it apart from the other iron-bound crates.

"The way for me to get back home is in that box?!"

Before he could answer a couple my girls rushed into the room. Molly was one of them, holding a gruesome lump of something bloody that I later figured out was the remains of a human arm.

"Time to go, Captain," Molly informed me.

"No, wait, we have to get this box out of here."

"No time, Captain!"

"Get him, at least!"

The three of us rushed the Doc and grabbed him, dragging him along behind. He fought back, but a couple of hits from Molly's disgusting club subdued him enough to come quietly.

We got to the topdeck and there she was, my ship, following us down. Argenta wasn't the only crew I'd left aboard. Eve flew the orny back and forth, ferrying my girls back to my ship. The surviving crew of the Syren had abandoned ship, overloading their few ornies. I even saw some hang-glider things disappear into the night sky. We were the last to leave.

But when Eve landed on the slanted topdeck of the Syren, and she saw Doc Sweetwater, my carefully crafted master plan went all to hell.

"FATHER?!" she screamed, confused and delighted, overwrought and overjoyed. She nearly jumped out of the orny, but the harnesses held her back. She started to untie them when Doc yelled out a bunch of words in a bunch of different languages. When he was done her face went slack, her eyes glazed over and she was completely still.

Doc shook himself free from my girls and ran to the orny, yelling at Eve in some language I'd never heard in all my time on this world. Eve's hands flew over the controls and the orny's wings beat faster, taking off without us.

I ran up to grab Eve, yelling her name. She didn't even look at me. Doc kicked at me as he climbed aboard, caught me on the side of the head. I fell back, and Eve took off.

Molly and another girl tried to hold on to the orny. Eve scraped Molly off on the Syren's railing. I never learned the other girl's name. She fell off the orny, tumbling through the night sky.

Just like we were.

Chapter Thirty Five

The Power of Friendship

I stared at the orny as it flew off, not really sure what had just happened. Some kind of post-hypnotic command? I didn't know, and as the ground rushed toward us faster and faster, I doubted I would find out.

Molly sat down on a pile of ropes. She'd dropped the bloody arm in her attempt to grab the orny, and now she reached over and picked it up. She looked at it briefly, then hurled it overboard.

Fighting the urge to vomit, I asked, "What was that?"

Molly looked at me, her eyelens irising and twisting to focus on me. "She took my arm, so I took hers."

"Anything else?"

"Ebonfury stopped me before I got her leg."

I offered her my hand. She looked at it, confused.

"Come on. Let's get off this ship."

"How? We have no way off."

"There's got to be parachutes somewhere, right?"

"I don't know that word."

I stared at her, stunned. "You're kidding me, right? A world of airships and no one invented the parachute?"

"So it is true? You're not from this world?"

"No, I'm not."

"That explains all your strange ideas."

"I guess. I just don't happen to think that women having a say in what they do with their lives, and not being slaves, isn't that strange an idea. Do you?"

Molly stared at me for a couple of long, precious seconds, then her glance lowered to my hand, still reaching out to her. She reached up and took it. "No, it's not."

"Come on, I think I know how to save ourselves."

I led her back belowdeck. Things had shifted around in the compartment where I'd found the Doc. Everything had slid forward as the ship tilted into the long slow nosedive, piled up against the windows. Molly and I had to climb down into the compartment and clamber over the crates.

We pulled up a couple of the heavy canvas tarps that had covered the crates and hauled them back to the topdeck. We tied ropes to the tarps' corners and then to each other. I explained to her how parachutes worked and hoped that the canvas wouldn't tear, hoped the wind would catch the makeshift parachute, hoped we weren't about to make a bad situation worse.

I mean, the Syren wasn't falling that quickly. Oh, it was definitely falling, but given the amount of time it was taking, it wasn't exactly plummeting. There was definitely a very slim chance we might survive the crash. But the chance of dying in the crash was infinitely greater, so I decided to try the parachute.

I took Molly's hand. She stared at me with her one human eye. There was fear there, but hope, too. She'd lost some of her rage for revenge. Hopefully I'd given her something more to live for.

I counted to three and we jumped.

For the record? Freefall? Still WAY not my favourite thing.

It didn't quite work out how I'd hoped, though. First, Molly's hand was wrenched from mine and we fell away from each other. When I tossed my tarp away from me, it didn't catch the air right away. Molly's caught, but I saw one of her corners come loose from the knot we'd tied. I fell further away from her, the ground hurtling toward me as the Syren hurtled away. I yanked on my ropes, willing them to disentangle. Suddenly the tarp caught some air and spread out, and the ropes tied under my arms hauled on me so hard and tight I was sure I'd broken some ribs. I fell slower, but still too fast. Molly passed me, moonlit terror shining from her face as she struggled with the ropes.

Then I heard a sound I will never forget. I swear I am not making this up.

The sky farted.

The biggest most terrible fart in the world.

I stared up and realized that my canvas had torn.

In less than a second I passed right by Molly.

I was going to die.

I know, I know. So how am I here telling you this story, right?

That's the power of friendship.

The connection I shared with Serena told her I had left the ship and and that I was falling through the night sky. Gigi had gotten the other orny, the one we'd bought at Djen, up and running. She and Tring, who had been paying a lot of attention to Eve, managed to figure out how to pilot the spare orny. And Argenta, without any word of an order from anyone, had chased the Syren down.

Argenta got our nameless ship under me just in time for me to slam into the balloon and slide off. Gigi and Tring got the orny under me just in time for Serena to grab the ropes. She had a hell of a case of rope burn afterwards, but they managed to keep me from smashing into the ground below.

My eyes scanned the night sky frantically as I dangled from the orny. Serena tied off the ropes and started hauling me up. I saw a glint of something metallic and pointed. "Molly!"

Serena stopped hauling and passed along my order to Gigi and Tring. They didn't bother with trying to coordinate with Argenta this time, they just flew straight at Molly, getting her parachute caught up in the landing skids under the orny.

We were saved.

Chapter Thirty Six

A New Name, A New Hope, A Beginning, An End

When we got back to our ship, nearly killing ourselves trying to dock in the launch bay, my girls hauled us up. I hugged everyone who rescued me, probably twice.

"We should see what salvage we can get from the Syren," Gigi said once she'd made sure the orny was squared away.

I looked down through the open launch bay doors. The Syren was sinking rapidly, headed for the desert mercifully far below us. It had seemed so much closer when it was hurtling toward me.

The Syren hit the ground. We couldn't really see it, the balloon was in the way, but when it hit it started dragging along behind the balloon, leaving a trail of destroyed airship behind it. Bursts of yellow light showed us where lamps exploded. And when the balloon finally hit, something must have sparked somewhere, some flame escaping the boilers or something, because the fireball was so incredibly huge and the explosion so loud it actually knocked us about. Then the superheated air created an updraft that knocked us around even more.

"Close the launch doors!"

Girls scrambled to follow my order, hauling on the lever. The launch doors closed and no one fell out. There wouldn't be any more deaths that day, not if I had anything to say about it.

I didn't actually have much say in the long run anyway. Nine of my girls died during the attack. Four more died from wounds they'd gotten, mostly because Eve wasn't there to save them. I had no idea what had happened to her, why she'd left with Doc Sweetwater, or where they would go. Eight more of my crew were injured enough that our two nurses felt they weren't qualified to judge if they might survive the week.

No one escaped injury, be they cuts, scrapes, bullet wounds, grazes, bruises, broken bones, and in Molly and Argenta's cases, dents. We all had scars from the fight, scars we would bear, in some cases, the rest of our lives.

I ordered us to land near the Syren's wreckage, upwind, not so close that we'd catch any flames or sparks from the burning hulk.

It burned through the night. I ordered everyone to get some rest. We were exhausted, we'd lost friends and comrades, but most importantly, we'd survived our first encounter as actual pirates fighting slavers. Today went in the win column, but not without cost. Part of me wondered if the cost we paid that night would ever seem equal to the gain we made. A ship of slavers had been destroyed, but some of the slavers had escaped. Would they return to piracy and slavery? Would they carry a grudge against us and hunt us down, like Tyr Ebonfury and Dr. Enerva? Captain Caliper said that there was an anti-slavery movement in the government. Maybe the former slavers would get out of the business. Maybe we would be a turning point.

So many questions plagued me as Serena led me to my quarters.

"Rest, Wal. Ve vill talk again at dusk."

"Hey, Serena?" I asked as she took my jacket off of me. That was when I noticed the bullet graze on my arm. I winced at the aches and pains I felt.

"Yes, Wal?"

"Why does everyone think I have a weird name?"

"Sunset is a time of change, a coming of darkness. People fear the dark, fear the unknown, fear change. That you chose such a name is ominous and portentous."

"Portwha?"

"It carries great meaning. And look, so many of those portents have come true. You led slaves in revolt, took over a ship, hunted down pirates. Allowed those former slaves the freedom to choose their own destiny for the first time in their lives, and I know that many of them liked it. The younger vomen in particular follow your example. Many of the older women vill forever regret the loss of their former lives, but the younglings, they vill never vish to return. As your name suggests, you bring change vherever you go."

I didn't hear most of that, though. She repeated it for me later. I was asleep even before my head touched the pillow.

We searched the wreckage the next night. Gigi claimed most of it a loss, but scavenged what she could. The girls kept busy pulling equipment and crates from the wreckage, sometimes still smouldering. I noticed that one of the crates had brass fittings.

I rushed over to where it stood. "Gigi, was this taken from one of the forward holds?"

She glanced at it. "Aye, Captain."

I checked the crate. It was the same crate the Doc said his portal was in, I was sure of it. I ordered it opened, right there in our launch bay.

Gigi and some of the more mechanically minded of my girls opened it in seconds. I looked at the equipment.

"Do you know what this is?"

Gigi gave it a thorough examination, picking apart pieces and inspecting them with a critical eye. "No idea," she answered after an eternity.

"Supposedly it's the machine that brought me here."

We'd had a ship's meeting and I'd explained that yes, what Captain Caliper had claimed was true. I came from another world. A world without institutionalized slavery, without airships, where women were able to vote. I'd answered their questions until they seemed satisfied. Then I called for a vote for captain. If any of them felt they couldn't follow a foreigner, they should feel free to fire me.

To a woman, they voted me back in. I'd breathed a huge sigh of relief.

Then we voted on something else.

After I'd thanked them for their vote of confidence in me, I looked at them all, each in turn, three dozen women and girls, my crew. "We've got no name and no figurehead for this airship. Now, in my world, we have an ancient legend, of these goddesses who exacted divine vengeance on evil men. They were beautiful and powerful and terrible in their fury. In fact, that's what they were called, the Furies." A piece of trivia floated to the surface of my mind. "The Furies were so terrible that people called them the Kindly Ones, just to keep on their good side. Now, I don't know if you have the same myths and legends on this world, and I see from some of your faces that you have no idea what I'm talking about, so I'm going to skip to the end and say, I propose we name this ship The Furies. Because that's what we're about, am I right? Revenging ourselves on the pirate slaver bastards who scour the skies and ruin lives, tearing mothers from their children, children from their parents, lovers from each other? We'll be The Furies, bringing vengeance against all the slavers out there. They'll learn to think twice about taking women as slaves. They'll learn to fear our names. What do you say?"

There wasn't a single vote against.

So, back to the Booty Hold. Gigi gave the unfamiliar machinery another thorough look. After an yet another eternity (that was probably closer to ten minutes), an eternity filled with feline muttering, she said, "I could maybe figure this out. But it's incredibly advanced. It might take me years."

"Better than never. Give it a shot. See what you can do."

We spent the rest of the night scavenging the wreckage for parts and spare supplies, transferring it all to The Furies. It was nearly dawn when we took to the air once more.

"Vhat vill you do?" Serena asked, stifling a yawn.

I sat back in the captain's chair I'd ordered installed in the wheelhouse. "Take every day as it comes. Maybe one day Gigi will figure out Doc Sweetwater's machine and send me home. Maybe not. I can't live my life based around a maybe. So, until that day, we'll sail the skies and see what we can see. There's a whole world out there to explore."

I stared out the windows of the wheelhouse and smiled. "Let's start with Libertia." I switched over to pure Anglic. "Argenta, set a course due east."

She turned the wheel. Serena smiled at me, put a hand on my shoulder, and left the wheelhouse.

The windows filled with the rosy glow of sunrise just over the horizon.

Other Series
by
Rob St.Martin

The Truthseekers Series

Welcome to Blackriver
Birthright
Level Up

***

The Princess Smith Saga

Princess Smith and the Clockwork Knight

***

The Squirrelman Books

Sins of the Past vol.1 - Calling All Crimefighters
Sins of the Past vol.2 - Endgame
The Amazing Adventures of the Sensational Squirrelman

ROB ST.MARTIN was born in Montreal, Quebec. A graduate of Concordia University, it took him years to realize he was a writer.

Rob's first published work (in an actual book, because he'd been publishing online for years before) was *The Mysterious Case of Spell Zero*, in Julie Czerneda's "Misspelled" anthology. Later he had the good fortune to collaborate with Julie on their Aurora Award-nominated anthology, "Ages of Wonder". His Squirrelman series has an international following, and rabid fans constantly clamour for more of his Truthseekers series.

Rob has had numerous mildly interesting and, in retrospect, generally amusing jobs. He lives with a wonderful woman he loves completely and three amazing kids who bring tremendous joy to his life. When not writing, Rob actively wishes he had more time to write.

Rob can be found online at www.talyesin.com.